Captured Heart

The Wolf Whisperer Series, Volume 2

Angeline Gallant

Published by Angeline Gallant, 2021.

CAPTURED HEART

First edition. November 27, 2021.

Copyright © 2021 Angeline Gallant.

ISBN: 979-8201351854

Written by Angeline Gallant.

Table of Contents

Chapter 1...1
Chapter 2...7
Chapter 3.. 14
Chapter 4.. 19
Chapter 5.. 25
Chapter 6.. 30
Chapter 7.. 36
Chapter 8.. 41
Chapter 9.. 47
Chapter 10 52
Chapter 11 56
Chapter 12 61
Chapter 13 66
Chapter 14 71
Chapter 15 77
Dear Reader, ... 84

Chapter 1

The stars still sprinkled the inky black sky, the world immersed in silence. Leaves whispered in calm, hushed tones as though sharing a secret before the heralding of a new day.

The women were the first to awaken, shifting wordlessly from below thick furs, withdrawing from the warmth of their husbands' bodies.

Greeting each other with a smile, words were not essential as Small Bird coaxed the fire to life. The men would be departing at daybreak, their meagre food supply sorely diminished. Their hunting party would rejoin the tribe at twilight if they were successful.

Chief Long Knife stood at the opening to the longhouse, observing the sun ascend over the hillside just above the treeline. Leisurely sunbeams expelled the final shadows of darkness away.

His wife, heavy with their first child, joined him breathing in the crisp morning air. She placed a gentle hand on her husband's sinewy forearm but didn't say a word.

Gentle Doe didn't need to tell Chief Long Knife she would yearn for him, or that she was proud of him and the leader he was to their people. Chief Long Knife didn't need to tell her how much he cherished her, having shown her completely the depth of his devotion.

At that moment they shared, Chief Long Knife tenderly caressed her extended womb. Eagerly anticipating the birth of their first child, he was certain she carried the next chief.

Silence.

Perfect silence, words unsaid enveloping the couple.

Pivoting, Chief Long Knife ate the corn mash Gentle Doe had brought him in no time, tearing off a chunk of the dried venison with his teeth. As he chewed, his eyes searched the tree line, a premonition something wasn't right settling on his spirit. There was no movement, yet he couldn't quell the feeling of sinister foreboding.

His people were famished, eating the last of their rationed food supply. Iroquois patrolled the waterways, yet they could not hide from their enemy indefinitely. With no alternative but to venture out, they prayed the Great Spirit would give them success. Without it, they would starve. The heavens had been closed up for weeks now, the ground as dusty as ash.

Chief Long Knife gazed down into Gentle Doe's mahogany-hued eyes, the silent exchange between husband and wife reassuring her of his love.

Without a word, he glanced over his shoulder at the men who had finished eating. Standing yet straighter, he gave Gentle Doe his empty dish, their fingers touching before leading the way to their waiting canoes.

As silent as a dragonfly hovering over the water, the men submerged their oars into the water, birch canoes gliding over the glistening waves. Arms flexing as they paddled, Gentle Doe watched until they faded from sight before returning to her people. There was much work to be done.

GENTLE DOE STOOPED over, her fingers delving into the dusty soil, probing thin roots. Most of the green shoots had turned brown, drooping underneath the unrelenting heat, unusually humid for this time of year.

They needed rain desperately. If the rain didn't come, they would have to move. Even if it rained, they would still likely have to keep moving, the Iroquois advancing from the East, forging into the Wyandotte Nation's territory.

A harmonious tribe, they did not seek trouble, instead, withdrawing from their deadliest enemy, the unrelenting Iroquois Nation.

Chief Long Knife, her husband, adhered to optimism, waiting for their village Shaman to pacify the Great Spirit into sending rain. So far, his best efforts had been to no avail. Perhaps Chief Long Knife would make his judgment after the birth of their child. It wouldn't be long now and time was running out.

The women worked side by side, children dashing about snagging their baskets and other small trinkets. The young ones believed that the one who could capture the most without being detected was the most quick-witted. The adults esteemed intelligence and those who were the most clever were particularly special.

Aquene called out a warning for the little ones to play closer, not so near the forest. With the men away... The children obeyed Aquene, their carefree laughter musical in the breeze.

Gentle Doe stood, massaging her lower back before reaching for her basket. A stew could be made from the few scraps of greens she'd managed to salvage along with the unusually small roots.

A movement from the corner of her peripheral vision was the only indication that something was amiss before the trees exploded with painted warriors on horses, many holding rifles. Their shrieks shattered the stillness, infusing dread into the hearts of the women and children who had been left behind.

Gentle Doe struggled to escape but was unable to see her feet beneath her sizable womb. Young girls screeched as they were swooped up off the ground. Their brothers, forcing themselves to be courageous, refused to show their captors the slightest indication of fear.

The children were shown mercy, flung unceremoniously onto the horses' backs, the invading warriors pinning them in place so there could be no escape. Older children rode behind, their limbs instinctively gripping their captor's hips. The children screamed for their mothers who fought back, tigerish in the face of fear.

Other women, unmarried or childless, ran, tripping on branches as they fled into the shelter of the forest. There could be no escape, Iroquois warriors claiming the women as they fled. They were surrounded.

A powerful arm swept beneath Gentle Doe's bosom, lifting her effortlessly off of the ground. The warrior kept her firmly in place in front of him, pinning her against his chest. Escape was hopeless.

ABANDONING THE VENERABLE and aged, the invading tribe set fire to the longhouse, the flames licking up the dry grass around it. A blazing inferno was the only evidence they'd visited the peaceful tribe before retreating within the forest. Flames crackled as they licked the sky, black smoke thick.

Gentle Doe blinked back tears. She wouldn't cry. Whatever her fate, Gentle Doe was the wife of a powerful chief. He would come for her and their baby. She needed to trust him and concentrate on surviving. The Iroquois, after all, was a merciless tribe.

Straight-back and defiant, she focused on the hand restraining her. His hand was smooth, brawny sinews just beneath his skin. Young, she assumed as his horse raced sure-footed between the dense foliage. At this break-necking speed, they would put too much distance between what was left of their home and wherever they were going.

Her captor relaxed his grip on her, allowing her to expand her diaphragm. Swallowing great gulps of air, tears burned her eyes.

The children and other women would need her to be courageous. Until the men rescued them, she was their leader and wouldn't be defeated now. Chief Long Knife would be proud of her.

Tucking her hands into the horse's mane, she attempted to conceal her emotions betrayed by her trembling fingers.

Gentle Doe knew the truth - she wasn't likely to see her husband again.

CHIEF LONG KNIFE LED his men as they returned with enough fish to nourish the tribe for the next few weeks. Instead of being greeted by their women and children, their home lay in ashes, the sound of mourning reaching their ears.

"Iroquois," those who survived the raid informed their chief.

Fish abandoned, the men ran into the forest, arrows drawn as they searched for the perpetrators of the crime. Hoofprints had trampled the parched grass pointing in one direction. East.

Returning to the charred clearing, Chief Long Knife indicated for his companions to make quick work of gathering what could be salvaged. With sorrowful hearts, they turned their faces towards the East.

It was time to fight fire with fire.

Chief Long Knife had waited too long, retreating from the Iroquois advances. Now they had his wife and child. There would be no more retreating.

A muscle clenched in his jaw as Chief Long Knife led the way toward enemy territory. The Iroquois had raided the wrong camp.

SETTING UP TEMPORARY wigwams, the Wyandotte camped on the shores of what is now known as Lake Ontario while the men raided tribes nearest the lake. In the evening they always returned with captives. Yet each night, Chief Long Knife returned without his wife.

Sitting in front of the fire, Chief Long Knife fixed unseeing eyes on the flames his heart tormented. He would not give up.

"We will raid again at dawn. This time, we will divide our number," Chief Long Knife indicated to the men sitting at his left side, "You go farther inland, and I'll lead these farther up the river."

There was no arguing with Chief Long Knife. Besides, they were hungry for revenge. Unable to find their wives and children, in this final raid, no mercy would be shown.

Revenge never tasted so sweet.

Chapter 2

Adelaide sprinted through the trees, her exposed feet nimbly skimming over fallen branches, moss caressing the underside of her calloused toes. Shoes were discarded as soon as the air turned balmy, promising the onset of summer.

Sunlight flickered through the dense forest as the young girl cantered toward the creek, the first sign of salmon splashing in the cool water, seeking their ancestral spawning ground.

Sitting on the shadowy embankment, Adelaide dipped her toes in the sun-sparkling water, breathing in deeply. Her sisters stood at the top of the steep cliff just on the edge of the clearing.

Arlana wore a dress meant only for dress-up. It had likely been a bridesmaid's dress at some point before it found its way from the second-hand store to being Arlana's most cherished possession. She stood in the sunshine, her baby sister at her side, long hair caressing her hips, quoting her favourite heroine, Anne of Green Gables. She'd read the book so many times, she knew it by heart.

Crossing her hands dramatically over her flat chest, she breathed in the shimmering rays bathing her upturned face. Daydreaming of none other than the handsome Gilbert Blythe, it was by far the most romantic love story she had ever read.

Arlana refused to step any further toward the edge of the embankment. It was much too steep and, if she placed her foot in the wrong position, she was certain she would inevitably plunge to an untimely death. Additionally, the trees were swarming with ants and spiders, mosquitoes dancing in the shadows. No, she was perfectly fine exactly where she stood.

Far below, her younger sister sat alone, daydreaming of the surefooted aboriginals who had once prowled this very hill, seeking sustenance from the jumping salmon in the creek. Adelaide had more in common with the stillness and the rippling creek than with her sister who recited prose, frightened of what lay within the forest.

The Gallen family attended their small, rural church like clockwork - twice on Sunday and never missing a Bible study or prayer meeting during the week. Their father, never late, opened the door waiting for his family to enter in a duck-like procession.

THEY WERE MUCH TOO early, the pastor and Sunday School superintendent the only ones who had arrived only moments before the Gallens.

The sisters walked down the cement stairs, their shoes echoing in the hush despite their efforts to be ladylike.

"Good morning," the snowy-haired Mr. McLeod smiled, locking a small chest where he kept prizes for any newcomers.

It was a very special cabinet that held small trinkets. The Sunday School children were aware that if they invited a friend to join them for Sunday School, not only would their guests get to choose a sticker or pencil, but they would as well.

"'Morning," Arlana murmured, straining for a fleeting look at the treasures within before Mr. McLeod fastened the door, twisting a small key in a padlock.

"You're early," he stated the obvious with a warmhearted grin.

It went without saying, they were perpetually early.

"Do you need help with anything?" Arlana offered, glancing at her sisters who stood at her side now in a horizontal, duck-like position.

If anything, the Gallen children knew how to be on their best behaviour.

"That would be great," Mr. McLeod accepted Arlana's offer. "If we finish before the others arrive, I will show you a book I brought today."

Curiosity piqued, the children worked quickly, ensuring the wooden chairs were in a straight line, row by row. Only three rows, however, as only a handful of children attended church, but one could never be certain if today, at last, there would be a visitor. It was better to be prepared.

Sitting down in the first row, the Gallen children peered over the ageing man's broad shoulders, examining the pictures of a book he clutched on his lap.

A missionary story! Mr. McLeod enjoyed regaling the children with stories of men and women who gave their lives to bring the Gospel to far-off lands. This story, however, promised to be different. Pictures of Native Americans captivated their attention. Mr. McLeod explained the book was about a missionary who was burdened for the souls of Canada's first people.

"I'd love to be a missionary to the Indians!" Arlana breathed, star-eyed.

Adelaide stepped back, frowning. Was this the same Arlana she knew? She crossed her arms over her chest, knowing the truth. Natives were the remotest thing from her sister's romance-filled mind.

At nine years old, all her sister talked of was Gilbert Blythe or on rare occasions, Civil War soldiers. An avid reader, Arlana seemed to imagine she would marry one of her book's heroes or a charming man from another era would step out of the pages of history and sweep her off her feet.

Arlana's mooning was rather pathetic.

Oblivious to her sister's glare, Arlana envisioned statuesque, bronzed warriors with muscled chests wearing only loincloths. She could easily lose her heart to such a man. Oh yes, Arlana would love to be a missionary or a captive. Either would be most romantic!

Mr. McLeod's eyes misted. At last one of the Sunday School children caught his vision. Arlana might just become the small Baptist church's first missionary!

Instinctively, he patted the girl's hand with his aged one, "I have booklets at home of missionaries living on Indian reservations. I will talk to your parents and drop them off this week for you to read. I am certain you will be inspired."

Arlana grinned. Anne of Green Gables already abandoned, rugged warriors in her place, Arlana already was inspired.

ARLANA SAT ON THE VERANDA balancing a four-inch-thick book on her scrawny kneecaps, eyes absorbing each word. In an ideal world, Arlana would do nothing other than reading. Okay, so perhaps she would still eat but only while she read.

A navy blue car pulled up in the driveway, Mr. McLeod beaming as he stepped out of the vehicle.

"Hello Arlana," he stooped to reach for the booklets laying on the dashboard, "I brought you the missionary stories I promised."

"Thank you!" Arlana breathed, excitement making her eyes gleam. She held out her hand for the dog-eared books eager to begin reading.

"If you have any questions, don't hesitate to ask. I've been supporting this ministry for many years."

Adelaide held the door open for their visitor before joining her sister. Arlana opened the first book, skimming the first few paragraphs before deciding to look at the pictures first. She held her breath, examining each photograph closely.

Believers stood holding Bibles, others appeared to be singing. In every picture, everyone wore contemporary clothing. There were no feathered headdresses, or buckskin and definitely no loincloth-clothed men. It was impossible to tell which of the men were warriors.

Disappointing did not adequately express the feeling Arlana experienced as she continued onto the next booklet. It was exactly the same as the first. There was a plausible explanation. Once converted, the natives shunned their traditional clothes, wearing instead of the clothing of white people. What a shame!

ARLANA NIBBLED HER lower lip, glancing up as Mr. McLeod bid her family farewell.

"Mr. McLeod, why are they all wearing clothes like us?"

"That is what they wear now and for many years it has been that way." He wasn't joking, his features sombre. "They need to hear the Gospel. I am so happy you are interested in taking the good news of Jesus to them someday."

Arlana looked away. She was the farthest from interested now. The idea was no longer fascinating or romantic, Arlana assumed it was because of missionaries that these Natives were no longer wild and fierce.

She waited until Mr. McLeod's car disappeared from view before gathering up the booklets.

"Here Adelaide, you can have them."

Arlana would have to figure out how to either avoid Mr. McLeod at church or tell him the truth: she no longer wanted to be a missionary. After a few moments, Arlana decided her only choice was to dodge the man she had always respected.

"I knew you weren't telling the truth," Adelaide frowned, clutching the booklets against her heart.

Arlana shrugged, "I wasn't lying exactly. I just thought they looked different."

Adelaide didn't understand her sister. Why should she? Adelaide's motives were true, her heart pure. In contrast, she genuinely cared about the First Nations people, unlike her sister who cared only if they were the same as the past - swoon-worthy. It was a blessing that Adelaide didn't understand her superficial eldest sister.

THE THREE SISTERS CROWDED into the tiny washroom, peering into the mirror as they prepared for church. Adelaide brushed her long, ebony hair until it shone like spilled ink. Arlana stood at her side, preening in case at long last, she might be noticed by one of the single men at church.

Years had slipped away since they frolicked in the country, yet their hearts hadn't changed, at least not that much. Adelaide wore her Sunday best as she prepared to meet with God, Arlana wearing her Sunday best hoping to find a Prince Charming who'd sweep her off her feet, still waiting for that elusive, *"And they all lived happily ever after."*

Jaira swiped Vaseline on her lips in lieu of lip gloss, eyes on their eldest sister. Dreaming of romance was far more tantalizing than their boring sister, Adelaide, who just didn't get it.

Adelaide glanced one last time at her reflection, satisfied that she looked as best as she could before leaving for church.

"Someone told me this week that I have wolf eyes," she sought Arlana's, biting her lower lip.

Arlana turned her deep blue eyes away from the mirror to look at her sibling. Adelaide was very beautiful with her gleaming hair and eyes that were neither brown nor gold, the colour of leaves in autumn sunshine.

Wolf's eyes.

Arlana shrugged, "No, you don't have wolf's eyes. They are seriously ugly."

There was no justification for being so cold-hearted. Cruelty dripped over her jealous words, but Arlana didn't care, aware that her sister's eyes were misted with tears.

Jealousy is a terrible thing.

Adelaide was different from her sisters. She was born to run with wolves.

Chapter 3

It is amazing how greatly time can transform the way people perceive things. At one time unimportant, add a sprinkle of time to it, and, in many cases, it is now valued.

Arlana never would have envisioned as a child that she would ever treasure her sister Adelaide so much. Jaira was a given, her "baby girl" and live doll, but Adelaide, they had never been close. Now, with time, Arlana had a new admiration for her peaceful sister. Adelaide was sensible and prudent with a kind heart, characteristics Arlana had never taken the time to appreciate in her younger years.

Now, each with a family of their own, the sisters had somehow or another found their way back to salvage the years that had been squandered.

"I was thinking of going for a drive," Jorken glanced up from his tablet, intruding upon Arlana's thoughts, "Is there someplace you'd like to go? It's supposed to be nice weather today."

Arlana nibbled the inside of her cheek. They didn't go for drives often, so this opportunity to choose wasn't something she was going to decide on casually.

"Would you mind taking us to the reservation? I'd like to go to the gift shop, and it is a nice drive. The cost of gas is cheaper."

Arlana threw in that tidbit of information as a "selling point."

Jorken took a while to respond, much too long for the impatient Arlana. Okay, so perhaps not as much had changed over the years as Arlana would like to admit, the virtue of patience still elusive.

"Ya why not," Jorken eventually decided, "Okay get ready, we'll leave in ten minutes."

Arlana strapped her child in his booster seat before passing him a small camera to keep him entertained on the drive. It took less than an hour to reach the reservation, farms scattered along the road. There would be abundant opportunities to take pictures of scenery he didn't see in Kingston.

Aziel took pictures, pointing out cows, horses and the occasional sheep as they drove along the twisting road. Jorken turned up the radio volume, but not too loud, allowing him to still speak over the country music playing on their local radio station.

"Why are you so quiet?" Jorken stopped to notice Arlana hadn't spoken a word since they'd left their apartment.

"I'm thinking," Arlana replied, eyes focused on the passenger window.

Notepad and pen on her lap, she strained to examine the name of the old burial ground on the side of the road, fractured, blanched gravestones sloped sideways.

"Those must be from the 1700s!" Arlana's voice was as animated as Aziel's.

"I'm not going to stop," Jorken didn't care that he hadn't been asked, "It's just weird you wanting to take pictures."

Arlana didn't bother to look at Jorken, after all, she might miss something whizzing past.

"They are forgotten," she explained, recording the name of the cemetery in her notebook. She'd research it later that night after her son was in bed. "Maybe they were Loyalists..."

Arlana pointed to a signpost at the edge of the road, bearing an image of Loyalists - just a silhouette, but it was sufficient. It confirmed that Arlana was on the correct track.

"Do you remember I told you about the Loyalists before?" Arlana called back to her son who was homeschooled.

"Yes, Mother, they were loyal to the King so had to leave America. Many came to Kingston where we live," Aziel grinned, recalling what she had shared with him on one of their walks in town.

"That's right! You've got a good memory," Arlana encouraged, "Did you see that sign? Can you imagine that the Loyalists may have walked along this road in search of a new home?"

"Maybe they rode on a horse, or a donkey," Aziel added, "Or a wagon."

Mother and son grew silent again, each lost in their thoughts.

Jorken shattered the silence, continuing to speak of goodness knew what, Arlana's thoughts in the portals of the past.

JORKEN SAUNTERED AHEAD, a slight limp in his gait, before disappearing within the white sprawling gift shop. It was the largest shop adjacent to the two-pump gas station. In front, an enormous wooden sculpture of a native was erected to stand sentinel outside of the Tyendinaga Mohawk reservation. Aside from the soft sounds of their shoes on crushed gravel was the crackling of a purple and white Mohawk flag, undulating in the crisp breeze.

Hand in hand, Arlana and Aziel followed Jorken from a distance.

"Don't touch anything okay? If something breaks, I'll have to pay for it," she cautioned.

The tapered aisles were lined with silver jewelry, artwork, carvings and beadwork. Toward the back, just off to the side, was a separate room with clothing and moccasins. Beyond that were housewares, soaps, maple syrup and nicknacks. Winding stairs led up to a loft containing priceless artwork but Arlana had never ventured farther than the first floor.

They'd depart for Kingston again as soon as they left the store, so Arlana took her time, examining each item slowly, wishing she were wealthy. Exquisite artifacts captured her attention, along with a painstakingly hand-painted canvas.

"Your Auntie Adelaide would love this place!" Arlana shared with her son, "She's always loved Indians. Let's look for a gift for her. What do you think she will like?"

Aziel immediately pointed to a doll wearing a traditional buckskin dress. Her reddish-brown cheeks were framed with two ebony braids, a feather in her headband.

"It's really nice," Arlana acknowledged, "But let's keep looking."

A leather necklace caught Arlana's eye. It wasn't the simple leather cord that caught her attention, but the pendant suspended from it.

Tenderly cradling the image in her hand, Arlana inspected it thoroughly. It was gorgeous and yet hard-featured at the same time, the impressive likeness of a warrior chiselled from silver.

How was such a thing even possible? The features were relatively rough-hewn, yet that could only be anticipated when working with such a hard metal. On the back, the artist had etched their signature, or perhaps, it was the name of the person the carving depicted. It was too difficult to read.

Arlana set it back down on the display table, turning away to resume her search for the perfect gift, but didn't take two steps before returning, lifting the necklace once again. There was something about it, and Arlana knew she would regret walking out of the store without it.

The metal was warm in her hand as they walked toward the cashier.

"I'll take this please," Arlana released the necklace reluctantly, placing it in the hand of the doe-eyed cashier.

"Ah..." she smiled softly, a glint in her fathomless chestnut-brown eyes.

Pocketing her change, Arlana extracted the necklace from the bag, cradling it in her palm on the drive home.

"What did you get?" Jorken glanced over.

Arlana revealed her single purchase to Jorken, her heart squeezing hoping he wouldn't criticize her decision.

"Hmph, that's different."

"I got it for my sister," Arlana explained, although it wasn't really necessary.

Chapter 4

A delaide was a busy, homeschooling mother to three children.

"Alright, you can take a quick recess," she called out, "I'm going to put the timer on."

The children weren't listening, dashing up the stairs, not wasting a second of their mid-morning playtime.

Pouring another mug of steaming coffee, Adelaide took a much-needed break, savouring the piping hot liquid before checking her email. She rapidly typed a response to Jaira, glancing at the time. Five minutes remained - enough time to check the mail.

Adelaide sifted through flyers, fingering the bulging frosted white package.

"We got a parcel!" Addy announced to the children who were reluctantly returning to continue their studies.

Adelaide turned off the timer with her free hand, reaching for the scissors.

"It's from your Auntie Arlana," she read the return address.

Three sets of eyes peered over her shoulder as she freed the contents: a pocket-sized gift box containing a necklace.

Adelaide didn't wear jewelry but this necklace was from her sister. Releasing it from the clear-topped container, she examined it a moment. It was unique if nothing else.

"Alright, let's get started."

Adelaide set down her half-empty mug on the corner of her desk, placing the necklace beside it. Necklace abandoned, she began to correct the children's work.

The fan oscillated, gently whisking the papers before her, creating a faint rustling against the desk. Standing, Adelaide searched the room for a paperweight, papers swirling on the desk before spilling onto the floor. Undulating they pirouetted, like a graceful ballet, the room spinning.

Adelaide should have grabbed some painkillers, her head suddenly throbbing. Reaching for a corner of the desk, the room swam out of focus, the sensation of falling washing over her.

A moment in time.

A CHILLY BREEZE WAFTED through the open windows of the small church that doubled as a one-room schoolhouse during the week.

Adelaide glanced around the room, swallowing hard. Her daughters sat on either side of her on the hard wooden pew, Joshua sitting at the end.

A handful of children sat beside their parents in their Sunday best frocks, the ladies wearing their best bonnets.

"Please turn with me in your Bibles to Luke chapter ten and we will read in unison verse two."

Adelaide didn't have her Bible with her. Her eyes narrowed as they focused on the pastor. A priest!

Like Dorthy in the Wizard of Oz, they clearly weren't in Kansas anymore.

"Therefore said he unto them, The harvest truly is great, but the labourers are few: pray ye, therefore, the Lord of the harvest, that he would send forth labourers into his harvest."

ADELAIDE SAT FLANKED by her children in the tiny chapel listening to the short, balding man. The priest wore an unadorned, sombre black frock, his long fingers clutching a well-worn Bible that had seen better days. A sizable wooden cross dangled from his neck, clacking softly against the wooden pulpit each time he leaned forward.

"Jesuit," Adelaide's mind recoiled.

She had been raised Baptist, her father having left the Catholic religion long before she was born, or so she had been told.

What was she doing sitting in a decidedly Catholic church?!

Peering about her, the small room was mostly filled with rugged men, several children, and even fewer women. The frontier was not an easy life for women, many perishing in childbirth or Indian attack Adelaide assumed, wishing she'd paid more attention to history. It would come in handy now.

The little man gripped the chiselled pulpit, leaned forward with an intensity in his eyes.

"There are over thirty thousand souls in this untamed wilderness who have never heard the sweetness of the Gospel of Jesus. Souls are facing a Christless eternity! Oh that God will burden each of us for these precious people! It is with joy and sadness that I bid you farewell. Tomorrow, I will leave with two of my fellow Jesuits for the inland territories. I cannot think of anything else and will have no peace until I bring these poor people the message of the Gospel."

His fervour for souls was stupefying. Adelaide had never entered a Catholic church and assumed they were wearisome, the priests speaking in monotone. This man was the opposite, his face contorted as he disclosed his inability to eat or sleep knowing souls were facing eternity without having ever heard the name of Jesus.

"Mom, we should go too," Isabella whispered, "and you could teach the children."

Adelaide nodded remembering her earlier yearning to reach the natives with the Gospel. Should she speak with this man after the service? Adelaide wasn't certain of the protocol, motioning with her hand for her youngest child to be quiet. It was disrespectful to speak during a sermon.

"If only one soul turns to Jesus, my work in this land will be complete. Just one soul snatched from the flames of Hell!"

Adelaide frowned. Yes, this man was radically different than what she had assumed, a thrill trailing down her spine at his impassioned words. A subtle stirring in her heart, yet it was too late. She was married now with children, complacent to walk with God and instruct her children to do the same. Mission fields were merely a distant desire, lost to the past.

The priest leaned even farther forward, displaying his balding head to the congregation.

"Farewell, my beloved brothers and sisters in Christ. I believe we shall meet again on Heaven's pearly shores. It is my prayer that we will answer the call of God, our hearts sensitive to His leading. The Bible says that we do not know what a day may bring forth. That has never been truer than in this land. We face constant dangers on every hand, but let us find grace to help us, to give us strength as we put our hope in God alone. May the peace and blessings of God be with you all, now and until we meet again."

After a short benediction, the congregation milled about, gathering their families as they made their way to the back of the humble sanctuary.

Adelaide clutched Isabella's hand as she and her children stepped out into the blinding late spring sunshine.

"Who is that man?" Adelaide asked a young woman who stood near her.

"You don't know? That's Jean de Brebeuf, of course," Marguerite lowered her voice, "He's been living among the Montagnais tribe for the past several months, but I heard he received an assignment directly from France to work among the Huron."

"He is being forced to go?" Adelaide raised an eyebrow, "I thought by his sermon he wanted to go of his own free will. He sounded so passionate about mission work."

Marguerite laughed, her low chuckle lighting up her eyes, "Of course he does! Brother Brebeuf cares for nothing but the savages. I don't believe it matters which ones as long as he is able to tell them about our Lord."

That made perfect sense.

"I was very surprised to see how passionate he is about sharing the Gospel," Adelaide revealed, "I never expected Catholics to care about such things."

"Hush," Marguerite cautioned, "You must not draw attention to yourself."

"PARDON ME?"

Marguerite gently touched her companion's elbow, leading Adelaide away from the chapel, "You are a Huguenot, are you not?"

The name sounded so familiar. Adelaide was confident she had heard her father or Arlana mention the name more than once.

"That's the opposite of Catholic?"

"You might say that. We are Protestants who have fled persecution in France. It is not easy for us here. We are forced to marry in the Catholic church and attend mass, but at least we do not have to pay for our faith with our lives. In that, we are blessed."

"Well, it's nice to meet you," Adelaide glanced over her shoulder uncertain exactly where she was supposed to go.

How was she to find the time-lapse portal, even if that is what it was that had transported her and her family to the past? It was a small comfort that she now knew at least one friendly face.

"I am so glad to meet a fellow believer as well, but please," Marguerite laid a hand on her new friend's arm, "Be careful who you talk with and be sure to come to mass."

"Come, you must join us for dinner," Marguerite grinned as her husband joined them. "Guillaume, this is my new friend...I'm sorry, I didn't even think to ask your name."

"Adelaide. It's nice to meet you."

The towering Frenchman smiled, his iridescent eyes flecked with hints of gold.

"Of course, we would love to have you join us."

The children followed close behind as Guillaume led the way, Marguerite's arm tucked in his.

Chapter 5

They sat down to a hearty meal of roasted root vegetables and venison, Adelaide and her children much too hungry to be picky.

Guillaume stood, leading those gathered around the table in a blessing over the food. The meal wasn't much, but it was sufficient.

"...May this food that You have provided, give us sustenance that we may be able to serve You better. Give us the strength to stand for You even on difficult days.

We would pray that You would be with our brethren back home. Give them courage and come to their aid speedily. Thank You for each of our guests gathered around our table. Bless each one. Guide their footsteps, and may they know You, our Great Redeemer Who is life everlasting. It is in Your precious and holy name we pray, Amen."

Guillaume brought his long-winded prayer to a close just as the steam spiralling from the vegetables dissipated. It would either be the perfect temperature or frigid, Isabella supposed, waiting until the giant of a man had pulled out his seat, joining them.

"Eat up!" He grinned, his chuckle, resounding.

They didn't have to be asked twice.

Marguerite's eyes sparkled as she picked up her fork, "They are one of us."

Guillaume glanced up, his eyes widening.

"Well, then you are doubly welcome at our table. It is good for you to have a friend Maggie," he beamed, glancing down at her calico-covered belly that had only just begun to show.

Women needed each other, it was just a fact.

"Do you live nearby?" He turned his attention back to Adelaide.

"I'm honestly not sure," Adelaide replied truthfully.

Would this gracious couple believe she had been thrust into their world via a gust of an oscillating fan? At the moment, Adelaide knew very little. Instead, she quickly changed the topic.

"I was surprised to see a priest, a Jesuit no less, so adamant about missionary work."

"Ah yes, you mean Jean de Brebeuf? He is passionate about the savages, there is no doubting that. I cannot fault him although, as you know, there is bad blood between our religions.

I am certain that he wouldn't hesitate to turn against us should we ever stand against the ruling that we must attend mass, regardless of our beliefs. Yet, in his burden for souls, he puts many of us to shame."

"Although," Adelaide frowned, "If they do not hear the truth of the Gospel, they are just as lost. I think it may even be worse as they will have a false sense of security believing they are truly saved, when in fact, it is a lie."

Guillaume nodded. Adelaide was correct and it was something he had contemplated as well.

"The issue is that those who know the truth are fewer in number and are yet to answer the call of God to reach the lost. If those with the truth will not go..."

"The fields are white unto harvest, but the labourers are few," Marguerite murmured.

Guillaume ran his hand through his thick, chestnut brown hair.

"Very few have ventured far, and those that have-"

"They were never heard from again," Marguerite leaned forward, sharing a haunting secret. "It is very dangerous to bring Christ into the woods."

"Jean de Brebeuf is right, My Love, someone has to."

The room was unusually quiet as each was left with their thoughts.

CHIEF LONG KNIFE SAT on the shadowy grass as the first shards of light permeated the trees promising a warm day. He didn't notice or care. Tormented, he prayed to the only one who could do anything to help him. In a moment of weakness, Long Knife allowed his Creator to see what others never would: Vulnerability.

CHIEF LONG KNIFE STOOD as he heard the soft rustle of his people stirring within the wigwam. An air of solemnity enveloped them as the men prepared to go on the warpath.

Gentle Doe would be found, and if not... He didn't want to complete the thought, refusing to lose hope. There would be a price to pay for his great loss.

The men assembled, paint smeared on their faces.

Intimidating.

Following Chief Long Knife's signal, they entered the woods in search of their enemy.

The hunted had officially become the hunter.

CHIEF LONG KNIFE ACKNOWLEDGED beyond a shadow of a doubt he would never see his wife again, and in turn, never gaze upon the face of their child. Battling his rage, he concentrated on the clearing

Trespassers.

The air was hushed save for the lone cry of a whippoorwill.

On the signal, painted warriors vaulted from the trees encompassing the log cabin. The inhabitants would be unsuspecting, and now, it was much too late.

Emitting a piercing war cry, the warriors didn't falter in their goal, seizing those who sought to escape.

There was no place to flee, no hiding place accessible as their homes were set ablaze. Those who managed to make it to the perimeter of the forest were captured as well. Horror and hysteria infused the atmosphere.

Desperation.

Adelaide clasped her daughters' wrists, uncertain where to run, yet adrenaline ignited her veins.

A split second later, a warrior wrapped his arm around her waist, wrenching her away from her children.

Adelaide screamed, gouging her captor's arms until she drew blood, kicking him with her legs, yet it was as though he were made of steel, unflinching beneath her best efforts.

Chief Long Knife glanced down at Adelaide's ebony head a moment before he secured her hands together, leading her along with the other captives toward their canoes, the children restrained as well. Draping Isabella over his bronze shoulder, he prodded the two older children ahead.

Tears blinding her eyes, Adelaide retained her gaze on her children. If she cooperated, would they be spared? It was worth the risk, the alternative something she wouldn't think of. Not now. Not ever.

By the second, it was becoming painfully clear there was nowhere to run

Maggie was slightly more fortunate, knowing the layout of their homestead.

Guillaume reached for his rifle, willing and capable of protecting his wife against the unexpected raid, yet he was no match for the band of warriors, noticeably outnumbered.

A tomahawk raised over his head, Guillaume knew the end had come. He watched in his peripheral vision as Maggie was dragged from her hiding place within the jagged limestone rock.

Guillaume prayed the savages would show his bride mercy, at that moment incapable of viewing them as souls, only barbarians. If they harmed her...

There was no time to think as he was bludgeoned with the backside of the raised hatchet, his world turning black.

The warriors wouldn't leave any bodies behind. What became of them, however, was another story.

They slipped away as soundlessly as they had appeared, fading into the shadows. Their canoes skimmed over the tranquil water as they withdrew from hostile territory.

The Wyandotte Nation did not pursue war, but they would strike back if provoked.

Looking out over their canoes bearing captives, they were pacified.

Chapter 6

Warriors stood opposite each other leaving a narrow path between the men brandishing war clubs in their upraised hands. Women stood amongst the men, a bizarre spectacle to the captives, the females also welding sticks and other sharp-edged objects.

"Run fast!" Falcon directed although none of the captives understood a word he said.

Shoving Guillaume forward, Maggie's husband staggered in an unsuccessful effort to maintain his balance, blood streaming from his head wound, sweat and blood blinding his eyes.

Scanning the group of natives, Guillaume searched for his wife a moment before being pummeled with clubs and the blunt end of hatchets.

Elderly women flogged him as hard as they were able with the sticks in their hands, unleashing their resentment and emotional pain on the man who had never harmed them.

Maggie grimaced, turning her head away from the scene. She simply couldn't watch as her husband was beaten.

Unflinching, Guillaume sprinted until he reached the end of the gauntlet, holding back a howl of pain as his fresh head wound was battered once again.

Chief Long Knife stood in silence, watching as Guillaume ran the gauntlet, his spirit starting to break although he refused to cry out or plead for mercy. Chief Long Knife admired the white man's stoic behaviour, yet it was not up to him to determine the man's fate. No, Guillaume's outcome lay in the hands of the women who had been left behind during the Iroquois' raid on their village. If they decided not to bestow mercy, his hands were tied.

Nodding at Chief Long Knife, Guillaume was re-bound and unceremoniously hauled off to the side. Maggie, Adelaide and the children were forced to watch as Chief Long Knife raised his knife and in one swift motion, pierced Guillaume's fingers vertically, carving through tendons and nerves until the blade of his knife contacted bone. Blood flowed freely, draining Guillaume's already pale features, yet he did not beg for mercy.

Chief Long Knife made certain Guillaume would never be able to raise a weapon against his captors. Wiping the man's blood off his weapon he stepped away without a backward glance, knowing what was coming next.

Black Crow seized Guillaume, binding him to a pole in the centre of their temporary village, a glint in his eye as one by one, he tore off each of Guillaume's fingernails. Guillaume paled, hanging his head as he experienced unimaginable torment, yet he didn't say a word.

Focus.

This world spun in front of his eyes as Guillaume forced his mind to focus on the sufferings his brothers were facing back in France. If they had the fortitude to die for their faith, surely he wouldn't give his captors any satisfaction as they mutilated his hands.

Chief Long Knife didn't participate, yet he didn't suspend the torture either. It was the custom of his people when they took male captives. They could have easily just scalped him back in the village, leaving Guillaume for dead, yet that would not have exacted the same level of vengeance they experienced now.

One outcry of pain and Guillaume could have ended it, meeting an abrupt death. His captors abhorred weakness and, disgusted, would have put a swift end to his life. Guillaume, however, was valiant, unflinching. The qualities were honourable, although still powerless to help him.

Leaving Guillaume bound to the stake, they turned their attention back to the women.

Adelaide's hands were constrained behind her back, making it impossible to shield her children's eyes from the gruesome spectacle they had been forced to watch. No mother would wish that upon their child, yet Adelaide was helpless.

Witnessing Guillaume's torture since he had been made to run the gauntlet first had the desired effect on the women. Tears flowed unhindered as they watched Guillaume's suffering, unable to hide their horror at what he endured.

Guillaume sought his wife's eyes, an expression passing between them. Their future looked most grim.

Adelaide attempted to prepare herself psychologically to run the gauntlet, and whatever would happen afterwards, yet how can one prepare for such a thing? She would endure for the sake of her children, then entreat their captors to show mercy to her offspring. The plan would only work if she were chosen before the children. A mother fiercely protective of her children, Adelaide's body surged with adrenaline. They'd rue the day they harmed her kids.

Instead of thrusting her toward the gauntlet, the warriors stepped back, making way for their chief.

Small Bird stood alongside Chief Long Knife, her features solemn. She pointed to Adelaide's children, Thunder Cloud immediately moving to their side. Without a word he led the three children toward the wigwam, propelling them inside. Guarding them closely, he waited for the ceremony to conclude.

Falcon strode to the front of the gauntlet, speaking in a low voice with their leader. Chief Long Knife indicated his approval.

Clasping Maggie's wrists, he led her toward the wigwam, Maggie casting one last glance at her husband.

She didn't dare fight back, biting her tongue. Falcon would regret claiming her.

Chief Long Knife motioned for Adelaide to be brought into the dwelling, joining her children and Maggie. The two women glanced at each other. Now they only had one another. If they played their cards right, they might be able to appease their captors then find a way to escape. One thing was undeniable: They would never stay in this godforsaken forest.

Guillaume was brought food and water, the ritualistic torture at last ended. He savoured the cool water held to his lips, gazing into the shadowy eyes of one of his captors, eyes that were unfathomable and...sorrowful?

A man without Christ, how could he know any better? Just maybe he was brought here to reach this man and the others with the Gospel. Guillaume's suffering, then, was for the sake of Christ and a small cost if even one soul could know the saving Grace of God.

More determined than ever, Guillaume hardened his jaw. For only one soul, this would all be worth it, Guillaume's heart echoing Brother Brebeuf's cry.

Guillaume, however, was not to see the longing of his heart.

FOR SEVEN LONG DAYS, Guillaume was tortured. They burned him slowly until chunks of flesh fell off his body, slicing his private parts until he was completely castrated. He fought cries of pain until he was almost certain he would bite his tongue off before losing consciousness.

The natives removed him from the stake giving him water and allowing him to rest.

Mercy?

Within a few hours, he was dragged back to the stake in the centre of the village, the inhumane torture continuing.

"One soul..."Guillaume breathed before singing in his native French tongue, "Jesus thou son of David, have mercy on me."

The song became the cry of his heart when he realized they were never going to let him live.

On the seventh day, he breathed his last, his final thoughts on the glory of Heaven that awaited him.

Chief Long Knife entered the wigwam, for once unwilling to participate as the men cooked Guillaume's remains before eating him, ingesting his life force.

Their numbers were greatly depleted from Iroquois raids and outbreaks of cholera. Guillaume had shown intense bravery and, in superstition, they absorbed his strength knowing in the morning, they once again would become the hunted.

The Wyandotte Nation could never be safe.

Chief Long Knife and Falcon did not allow their women and children to step out of the wigwam until no trace remained of the Frenchman. It would be easier this way for them to adapt if they never knew.

The Iroquois women who had been taken captive on the first raid exchanged looks, knowing full well what happened to captives. After all, it was their own nation that was known for even greater brutality. They glanced over at the pale-faced women who huddled together, their eyes relaying a message:

Welcome to our world.

If they wanted to encroach upon their land, they would face the same fate as Native captives had for centuries. It was nothing personal.

"Come," Small Bird smiled, motioning the shy women to join her, "It is time for you to become Wyandotte."

They hesitated, uncertain what she was trying to say.

Other elderly women stood, placing their hands on the pale-faced women's arms, guiding them down to the river, their source of life. Removing their clothing, they were scrubbed hard until their skin turned bright pink.

The men had withdrawn into the shadows of the trees, affording the women privacy. Only Dark Cloud remained in the entrance, his eyes watching the children's every move. Iroquois children who'd been taken captive crouched beside Adelaide's children, refusing to let fear show in their wild eyes. This was the way of their people. It must be accepted with bravery. Their mothers would return from the river, Wyandotte.

Chapter 7

The rippling water tinkled like tiny bells. Maggie stared straight ahead with unseeing eyes, unaware of the first shoots of green grass lining the lakeshore or the sunlight which glinted off the rippling water.

Her stomach lurched again, her arm held over her mouth as she tried to suppress her dry heaves. The trauma of the past week didn't help matters. Unaware that her husband's bones lay in a shallow grave near the clearing, Maggie watched and waited for any sign of her husband.

Adelaide assumed he may have been sold as a slave, traded, or best yet set free. It was too strange that they had never seen him again. Adelaide hoped for the best, but Maggie's intuition was quite the opposite.

Falcon had escorted her into the wigwam her first day in the village, motioning to a pile of furs covering a raised platform. She quickly learned that this was to be her sleeping quarters and where she would remain, guarded by the imposing warrior who scarcely uttered a word.

Occasionally he left, but never for long and when he wasn't there, Small Bird or another woman took his place, keeping a watchful eye on the woman who wasn't able to stray far.

Adelaide, on the other hand, was kept with her children and was given more freedom, if it could be called that. She too was unable to leave the confines of the wigwam but was permitted to venture as far as the fire in the heart of the dwelling and approach the other dark-skinned youngsters who studied her with wide eyes. Perhaps it was because Adelaide had young ones that she was trusted more.

A mother wouldn't leave her children.

"You must eat something," Adelaide whispered, holding a dish of steaming broth that reeked of fish.

The odour caused Maggie to lose the contents of her all but empty stomach, gaining the scrutiny of more than one of the matronly women within the longhouse.

Aquene clucked her tongue, helping scrub the mess, ignoring Maggie's cheeks, flushed scarlet.

"I'm sorry," the young brunette murmured, but it was pointless, the only one understanding also helping clean up the evidence of her companion's frailty.

The women weren't foolish. They'd been around long enough to see that the natives despised weakness. Fear clutched at their hearts, the women unaware of the consequences should they break rules they didn't yet understand.

Food couldn't be wasted, so Adelaide passed the dish to her daughters who shared the simple meal.

"If you don't eat, you'll waste away," Adelaide rubbed Maggie's back, "We need our strength if we are to escape."

The language barrier only worked in their favour.

Chief Long Knife had taken a special interest in Adelaide although he, like the others, rarely spoke. A slight nod appeared to be sufficient, yet Adelaide had caught him watching her more than once.

It was unnerving, yet she was determined to prove she could be trusted. A little more freedom was all they needed to make a break for it. At this rate, Maggie wouldn't make it far.

Small Bird appeared to hold the most weight among the women. Turning her attention to the ageing woman, Adelaide motioned with her hands in a cupping motion then brought her cupped hands to her mouth before pointing to Maggie.

Frowning, Small Bird rose, speaking to Falcon who sat nearby, vigilant as always. Small Bird clutched Maggie's arm, motioning Adelaide to follow.

The children refused to be left alone in the longhouse, stepping out for the first time into the blinding sunshine.

Now Maggie knelt on the edge of the river, gazing down with unseeing eyes at the shimmering water. One tip forward was all it would take for her to be swept away, unable to swim. It would be so much better than having to return to her captors. Just one little thrust forward...so why did she hesitate?

Cupping her trembling hands, Maggie slowly brought them to her parched lips, the warm sun caressing her ashen features. She blinked back unbidden tears.

Maggie needed to believe her husband was free. If she didn't pull herself together, all that remained of her husband would perish, and that is something she would never forgive herself for.

Straightening her slender shoulders with a renewed resolve, Maggie dipped her hands into the refreshing water once more, drinking deeply of the life-giving source.

Adelaide glanced over at her friend and smiled, noticing the glimmer of determination in her friend's dusky eyes.

FALCON WAS NOT A NATURALLY cruel man. In fact, the Wyandotte Nation was one of the most civilized of the Eastern Tribes. He never would have gone on the raid if his wife had not been stolen in the unprovoked Iroquois attack. Nor yet would he have ever taken a captive if he did not need to replace what he had lost.

Had Maggie looked past his stoic exterior and met his eyes, she would have seen gentleness in their charcoal depth. Love was not something he intended to force. The truth was, he didn't expect to ever love anyone as much as he had Sweet Song.

Falcon looked away, hiding even a trace of emotion at her memory. They had only been married a month before...but had grown up together as children. He'd wanted to marry Sweet Song for as long as he could remember, seeking to impress her with his bravery since they were young. No, Maggie would never match up to Sweet Song, but his wife she was.

No one would challenge his claim to the young woman, most of the other braves having chosen Iroquois women as replacement brides. Chief Long Knife was the other exception, his watchful eye on Adelaide.

As for Adelaide, it didn't take more than a day for her children to instinctively recognize Chief Long Knife's authority, watching from the shadows how the adults interacted with each other. Chief Long Knife was clearly the leader, yet Small Bird's whisper was the only thing that would stop him in his tracts. They assumed she was his mother, Joshua empathizing with the stoic chief.

The women and braves treated the children with kindness, fussing over them. They were served first and given small treats, toys that were hand-carved and for the girls, corn husk dolls.

Gnarled hands braided the girls' hair as the elderly women softly hummed a melody the children couldn't understand.

It was an unusual feeling to be doted on by the same people who had snatched them from all they had known, burning their homes.

Love overcoming fear.

The Iroquois children were the first to relax, joining the adults in activities that were somewhat familiar. Within the week, the children moved freely in the wigwams, the first to be trusted to step out into the sunlight. They wouldn't go far, unwilling to leave their mothers.

Joshua joined the other boys in their rough play, his quick mind learning a few new words. His attempt to speak the words he learned was met with smiles and playful giggles, the adults smiling their approval.

Chief Long Knife watched Joshua's attempts to accept his new life, a hint of a smile tugging at the corners of his lips when no one was looking. He set down the stick in his hand, motioning for Joshua to approach him. Pulling a small knife out of a pouch hanging from his waist, he showed Joshua in slow motion how to whittle the stick, small curls of wood falling at his feet.

Joshua tried imitating Chief Long Knife's movements, although he was far more klutzy in his first attempt.

"Aoo," Chief Long Knife nodded.

"Aoo," Joshua repeated, noting the sparkle in Chief Long Knife's eyes. Pride.

Joshua's grin showed it was enough as he hunkered down beside the tribe's chief, wielding the small knife in his hand. He worked quickly, cutting off large chunks of wood.

Chief Long Knife held out his hand, guiding the boy's showing him again to work slowly, taking pride in his work.

"Aoo," Chief Long Knife repeated again.

Yes.

Small Bird stood unnoticed in the wigwam entrance watching her son and new grandson.

At that moment she saw only hope for the future.

Chapter 8

Aquene helped Maggie don a beautiful, white buckskin dress, delicate beadwork adorning the bodice. Small Bird held out a similar dress to Adelaide instructing her to dress with a gesture.

The women looked at each other noting the Iroquois women were also dressing in the white buckskin. Neither woman protested, allowing their hair to be smoothed until it shone before a bone comb was worked into their long hair.

The older women stood back, admiring their handiwork, their smiles brightening weather-worn features.

They spoke softly in a language that was both guttural and musical at the same time.

Aquene stepped out of the wigwam moments before the men followed her into the smoke-filled interior, the men dressed in white buckskin as well, faces decorated in red paint. Porcupine quills and feathers adorned their glossy black hair.

Maggie and Adelaide stood holding baskets containing cakes made from cornmeal with dried fruit, the women prodded forward, given baskets containing folded shirts and cloth.

Adelaide and Maggie exchanged a look before glancing over at the Native captives beneath lowered lashes.

In turn, the men spoke soft words the women didn't understand. The Natives, however, seemed to understand what was being said, repeating similar words.

Adelaide looked between Small Bird and the Native Women before glancing up at Chief Long Knife. She could be mistaken but his expression was almost tender.

Setting their baskets down, the men began to dance and sing, the women joining in before, one by one, each of the couples dressed in white buckskin retreated to the shadowy corners of the wigwam after the sun had disappeared for yet another day.

Falcon led Maggie back to the side she had stayed in since their arrival, but led her past her bed to his sleeping quarters, pulling her gently down onto the furs beneath him.

Small Bird rounded up the children, guiding them to her side of the enclosure. She clucked softly as they peered over their shoulder at their mothers, confusion mirrored in their eyes.

Chief Long Knife held out his hand to Adelaide, guiding her to his sleeping quarters, the reality of the situation suddenly hitting her squarely in the face.

This was it.

Chief Long Knife held her hand firmly, striding toward his bed with determination.

Realizing what was about to happen, Adelaide attempted to pull her hand away, but he held her with an iron-like grasp, pulling her down onto the furs.

"I'm married!" Adelaide protested vehemently in the darkness.

Leaning over her, he pulled the furs over their shoulders.

Closing his eyes, Chief Long Knife breathed in her scent. He could not forget Gentle Doe so soon but his mother was correct. They needed to move on, leaving the past behind them. His hand tenderly stroked her arm, his thoughts distant.

The chief believed he could love Adelaide in time, but if he had the choice, his heart needed more time to heal from his loss. He would go through the motions, but his heart was far away, in the hands of his first wife.

It was a shame Adelaide couldn't read her new husband's thoughts as she twisted beneath his weight, wrenching her body away from him. Facing the thatched wall, she held her breath, praying Chief Long Knife would take the hint and leave her alone. She had clearly run out of time to plan their escape.

Sighing, Chief Long Knife laid down on his back beside her. There would be other nights. Clearly, both needed to mourn their losses longer. It was enough that they were bound together as husband and wife.

Surely, now, his mother would be satisfied. He had obeyed her and remarried. Adelaide brought children with her, giving her grandchildren. Before the year was over, they would have a son who would one day be chief regardless of having a pale-faced mother.

Chief Long Knife was fond of Adelaide's children and assumed her husband had died at some point from one of the many plagues the pale-faces had brought with them. Little did he know Gavin was at work, having missed the wind that had catapulted his family into the past.

Chief Long Knife lay awake long after Adelaide's breathing had slowed, her body twitching in a restless sleep. He reached out, drawing her against his side, protecting her from the night terrors that had come. Only secrets lay between them and the knowledge he was the cause of her horror-filled dreams.

Brushing his lips against her soft hair, he closed his eyes, deciding to leave her alone for now. She would trust him in time. When the nightmares no longer tormented her, then he would show Adelaide he was a good husband. By then, just maybe his heart would be healed as well.

THE MEN SLIPPED OUT of their beds before dawn, leaving only the women and children behind with the exception of Thunder Cloud who stood guard. Chief Long Knife wasn't ready to leave the women defenceless again. The last raid was much too fresh in their minds.

Aquene and Small Bird had woken before the men preparing their breakfast, their voices raised scarcely above a whisper.

Chief Long Knife ate in silence, yet that was nothing unusual. The food supply was getting low with the additional mouths to feed. After last night, Chief Long Knife was anxious to be back on the water, the fresh air clearing his hazy thoughts. Scraping up the last drop of corn mash, he stood, waiting for the others to join him.

Small Bird noticed her son glance back over at Adelaide, sound asleep underneath the furs he had thoughtfully arranged over her pale shoulders before slipping silently out of the bed they had shared. As dawn approached, she finally slept serenely, the nightmares dispersing with the arrival of daylight.

"Light chased away the darkness," Chief Long Knife's spirit mused, contemplating the deeper meaning.

Falcon hunkered down alongside his mother, offering her a larger portion of dried fish.

She held her hand up, rejecting his offering.

"You will not be returning until nightfall," her excuse.

Aquene knew none of the men would eat again until they returned, requiring the nourishment more than she.

"My woman is already with child," Falcon pronounced, his voice hushed so the women and children would not be awakened.

Aquene nodded. That would explain Maggie's constant bouts of illness. Rather than it being a shame, the thought of another baby being added to their midst was a source of great joy, Aquene's face erupting in a smile although the baby was not her son's. It did not matter, the child was already recognized as Wyandotte and claimed by his stepfather. No one thought of the baby's father they'd butchered only a few days ago.

"We will take greater care of your wife while you are gone," Small Bird spoke first as she joined her sister and nephew, "It is time these women learn our ways and speak our language."

The Iroquois women already spoke their language so their concentration would be given to the pale faces.

"You have done well," Aquene beamed, already thrusting out her chest with pride.

The raid had been successful, she was the first to become a grandmother.

They watched as the men disappeared over the horizon before turning back to the fire, preparing a fresh breakfast for the women and children who were stirring in their beds.

Maggie sat up, brushing long strands of ebony hair from her face. Flushed as pink as an English rose, she touched her kiss-swollen lip, avoiding Adelaide's eyes. What had transpired was not something any of the women wished to discuss. It was their fate, nothing more. Maggie, however, was torn between her betrayal of her husband's memory and the remembrance of being cradled in Falcon's muscular arms as he had tenderly convinced her that she could most definitely learn to love again. What would Adelaide think of her fickle heart?

Gently stroking the fur that was still warm from her husband's body, she savoured the lingering memory of her wedding night before sliding her feet onto the floor. Every one of the young women had experienced the same fate, so Maggie straightened her shoulders as she stepped toward the fire hoping Adelaide wouldn't mention it.

There was a strained, uncomfortable shyness between the two women as they huddled around the fire eating a small dish of mashed corn

Aquene smiled, or more accurately, beamed down at Maggie, cooing over her as she held out a dish of corn mush. She gestured toward the platter of dried fish, shaking her head "No," before resting her hand on Maggie's womb.

She knows.

Maggie's face flushed a deeper rosy tint witnessing the joy radiating in the older woman's eyes before focusing on her golden-hued breakfast.

Adelaide and the children joined her, deciding it best to keep her secret to herself - she was the only woman who had made it till morning untouched.

Why she couldn't understand but was more than grateful. She'd woken up once in the night, discovering herself held tight, her head resting against Chief Long Knife's heart. Blanching, she hadn't struggled, more fearful of waking the chief up than she was at being held so close to the man who had led the raid and been the first to torture her friend's husband.

It might feel oddly comforting to be enveloped in his powerful arms, yet it was clear as day Chief Long Knife was a savage that could not be trusted, least of all, with her heart.

There was only one answer. They must escape. With the men away, today looked promising.

Now, to get Maggie's attention.

Chapter 9

They made quick work of their breakfast, the village patriarchs leading the women and children out into the dawn.

The younger women followed the older ones' lead, holding woven baskets against their hips, as they entered the forest. Plump mosquitoes buzzed around their ears yet the elder women didn't seem to be affected by the blood-thirsty insects, nor their Native counterparts for that matter it would seem. Clearly, the pesky insects preferred European blood, Adelaide thought ruefully swatting them away with her free hand. Undeterred, they returned within seconds, buzzing around her neck.

Small Bird looked up, cocking her eyebrow at her daughter-in-law's vain attempts to thwart the swarms of mosquitoes that had joined them. The secret to their not being eaten alive by the parasitic bugs was their smoke-scented bodies, the smoke from the fire creating an unappealing barrier between them and the mosquitoes. The younger women hid their grins. Adelaide and Maggie would be preparing supper tonight.

Distracted, Adelaide wasn't paying attention to the other women, her basket all but empty. She reached for a cluster of shiny red berries, tossing them into the basket.

"Stan!" Small Bird reached into her basket, pulling out the strawberry-red cluster of fruit. "Stan!" she repeated again before tossing the berries onto the ground.

Well so much for that, Adelaide frowned.

"Aoo," Small Bird snapped off a cluster of deep blue berries, replacing the ones she had taken, then pointed to her own basket of dark blue fruit.

Adelaide flushed. It was painfully obvious she hadn't heard a word of the lesson.

Isabella giggled, popping a berry Small Bird held out to her into her mouth.

"Oh, Mom!" Isabella giggled again around the juices

flowing from the fruit.

Small Bird smiled, patting Isabella's blonde hair before continuing to gather fruit.

"Maggie, we have to leave today," Adelaide lowered her

voice, noticing with chagrin how full Maggie's basket was. Was it only her who had clearly slacked off?

"Are you sure? Where will we go?" Maggie frowned.

"You don't want to stay here now do you? We don't belong here. It is our only chance with the men away."

Falcon.

Maggie swallowed hard around the lump in her throat but nodded.

Adelaide whispered in Joshua's ear, his face contorting into a scowl, but he did as he was told, stepping backwards, his hands on his sisters' arms.

Small Bird and Aquene spoke quietly, the other women joining into the conversation as they slowly moved down the line of trees, harvesting food for the tribe.

It was painfully obvious they didn't belong. If they could escape, Adelaide was one step closer to returning back to the future. If only she could find that little church, she was certain she would be able to be transported back to the comforts of the life she had taken for granted.

Distracted, it was now or never. She'd seen where the men left the canoes and had used one before, going out on the lake with her aged father. It couldn't be that hard to get away - not if both canoes were gone. Surely these women wouldn't swim after them and even if they did, they would never be able to keep up.

"Now," Adelaide breathed a moment before she and Maggie stepped back into the thick underbrush making their way back to the encampment before the others. The canoes lay within view.

"Help your sisters!" Adelaide instructed Joshua who had jumped into one first, reaching up to lift his slender siblings into the canoe behind him.

It had been so many years since Adelaide had run, her footing sure as she descended the steep embankment towards the creek, yet, it was as though her spirit remembered, propelling her forward as she dragged Maggie behind her, fingers encircling Maggie's slender wrist.

"We'll find your husband," Adelaide encouraged her to run fast, but only made Maggie blanch.

How could she face Guillaume after what she had done last night?

THERE WAS NO TIME TO think as she tumbled down the hill headfirst, landing in the deep water with a splash.

The fact Maggie might not be able to swim was something Adelaide hadn't taken into account.

Dark hair swirled over the surface of the water, before Maggie sank, her arms and legs flailing wildly in a futile attempt to learn how to swim when it was much too late. Her long dress wrapped around her legs, weighing her down.

Adelaide watched helplessly as Maggie's head slipped beneath the water for a final time, she and her children unable to save their new friend. Adelaide cried out in utter helplessness.

Regret.

THE RAPIDS WERE TREACHEROUS, tossing the crudely made canoes up and down, Brebeuf's stomach reeling in objection, yet he bit his tongue, refusing to disclose his secret: he couldn't swim.

"There is too much weight," his younger comrade shouted, most un-priestley, passion enveloping each word.

Panic.

Hands clutched Brebeuf's sack, casting it unceremoniously into the raging water. A splash and his possessions were gone, whirled away in the white rapids. Brebeuf didn't have time to think, as the canoe capsized.

What became of his companions, Brebeuf could not know, his head submerging beneath the frothy, merciless water. Sputtering, his head bobbed up and down in the water which filled his mouth and lungs as he thrashed, his black cloak rising in the water, exposing pale ankles to the fish.

It was an embarrassment that his quest to win souls had met with such a fate mere miles from the fort. Washed ashore, he would likely never be located, and as for his writings...

Blackness overcame him as he sank to a watery grave.

Chief Long Knife vaulted out of his canoe, plunging into the water as the balding man sank beneath the waves like a dead weight. Muscles rippled, glistening wet beneath the sun as he disappeared into the depths, wrapping his arm around the black-robed man who was about to breathe his last.

Secured, Brebeuf was hauled out of the water, then dumped unceremoniously into the canoe before the meticulously crafted canoe whisked him along the swirling water.

Chief Long Knife skillfully maneuvered the canoe past the water the palefaces had been unable to traverse.

European life had done nothing to prepare Brebeuf for this wild country.

Brebeuf sputtered, eyes widening as he caught his ragged breath, taking in Chief Long Knife's broad back as he gripped the oars. Brilliant sunshine glistened off his damp hair, water droplets trickling down his taut back muscles.

Brebeuf had not found the savages, they'd found him.

They rode in deafening silence, Brebeuf grateful to his rescuer, blissfully oblivious of their barbaric nature evidenced just days earlier.

If Brebeuf knew, perhaps he would have jumped back into the raging river.

Thunder Cloud paddled at the back of the canoe, his eyes narrowing on the man they had delivered from certain death.

Pale-face.

What was he doing this far inland?

Thunder Cloud didn't trust the advancing Europeans and had good reason although it was only a forewarning he couldn't shake.

Glowering, he jabbed Brebeuf in his bony back indicating his ragged shoes. He gestured twice, showing Brebeuf that he needed to remove his shoes. The birchbark canoe was too delicate.

Obediently, Brebeuf removed his shoes, peeling the skin off large water blisters. Sticky blood covered his toes, oozing over his bandages.

Thunder Cloud looked away.

Chief Long Knife glanced back over his shoulder, raising his fist in the air. He called out, signalling that they were cutting their fishing expedition short, turning the canoe towards home.

Chapter 10

Chief Long Knife wasn't anticipating seeing his children huddled in a canoe or his wife half-hanging out of the second, features ashen as she reached into the water. Immediately he knew something was wrong.

A second later, Falcon howled, leaping off his canoe, before sinking beneath the waves. A few minutes longer and Falcon would have been a widower instead of a bridegroom.

Thunder Cloud remained in the canoe with Brebeuf as Chief Long Knife launched out of his canoe and into Adelaide's with his long legs, alighting behind Adelaide with the agility of a deer. He wrapped his arms around her, lifting her to shore while reaching for the children's canoe with his free hand.

Joshua didn't have to be ordered, jumping out of the canoe before reaching for his sisters, hanging his head as he stood beside the chief. He needn't have worried, Chief Long Knife recognizing this escape attempt wasn't his doing.

Chief Long Knife glared down at Adelaide's head. He'd been too soft on his wife and she had taken advantage of his weakness. He'd deal with her later, he vowed, watching Falcon come to shore, a soaking wet, sputtering Maggie in his arms. He frowned, looking at Adelaide who had carelessly risked her friend and the baby's life. Were they so terrifying that she had felt the need to run and most assuredly lose their lives had they not shown up just then?

Thunder Cloud's thoughts were dark, but he kept quiet, knowing better than to criticize his chief's bride.

Chief Long Knife emitted a mournful cry as Thunder Cloud climbed out of the canoe, dragging Brebeuf behind him.

The women stepped out of the forest, unaware that the children and women had escaped.

Aquene ran to her son's side, hand covering her mouth. Not a word was said as she embraced the younger woman, bringing her into the warmth of the wigwam.

Small Bird followed, frowning at Adelaide, yet Chief Long Knife didn't release his hold on his wife. Turning to the children, Small Bird motioned for them to follow her back into the wigwam, first stopping to pick up Maggie's nearly full basket of berries.

The children hung their heads, ashamed at their display of ingratitude in the face of the kindness they had been shown. If it were up to them, they would never attempt another escape.

Adelaide's eyes blazed as she watched Brother Brebeuf brought to shore. He was the same man who had spoken passionately of his love for the natives' souls.

A look of recognition passed between them before he was dragged off, the warriors already forming a gauntlet. Yes, it would have been better if Brebeuf had met a watery death.

Chief Long Knife half-dragged Adelaide to the front of the wigwam, facing the end of the gauntlet Brebeuf must face. Tightening his grip on Adelaide's pale flesh, he signalled with his hand for the attack to begin as Brebeuf was thrust forward.

Brebeuf focused on the teary-eyed woman in the chief's arms as he ran, stumbling as a rock tore into his bloodied foot.

Adelaide reached for him as he fell forward at the finish line, but was yanked backwards against her husband's chest.

On his knees, Brebeuf remained, head bowed, blood pouring from his feet.

"Let him live!"

Adelaide half-twisted in her husband's arms, speaking a language he did not understand.

Looking into her reddened eyes, tears streaming down her cheeks, Chief Long Knife lowered his hand. The man prostrating just past her shoulders would be spared. A wedding gift for his bride, although she didn't deserve it.

Love. It was a strange thing.

Groaning in frustration, the young braves raised Brebeuf from the ground, guiding him into the lodge. They indicated a spot near the fire where he could warm himself, children peering shyly behind their mothers.

Joshua smiled at the familiar man who had spoken so passionately about his love for these people. Now Joshua understood the sermon. He inched closer to Brebeuf, smiling.

Brebeuf glanced at the blonde, blue-eyed captive, but said nothing, only a small glimmer in his eyes indicating that he recognized the youth.

CHIEF LONG KNIFE SAT across from Brebeuf, pulling Adelaide down between him and his mother, motioning Joshua to sit at his other side.

"Demon," he murmured to his companions, eyeing Brebeuf's black robes.

Evil had come to their village, clothed in black.

"The white man has sent a demon to us for taking their women and children. We must leave in the morning."

Falcon and Thunder Cloud nodded. It was time to flee once again.

Chief Long Knife glanced over at Adelaide. They'd cover many miles before this time tomorrow. She would be a fool to try to escape again, only raiding Iroquois parties between where they were headed and her old home.

She would never make it back to the fort alive. Unfortunately, he wasn't so sure Adelaide wouldn't take that risk. In that case, he would make her love him. Once she loved him, she'd rather die than leave his side.

Chief Long Knife's eyes twinkled as he turned his focus back to the demon in their midst. An evil presence, yes, but they would take him with them. If they let him go now, he could easily lead more of his kind to their village. No one was willing to take that risk.

"More fish?" Small Bird held out the platter to Brebeuf.

"Thank you," Brebeuf breathed, "Thank you for your kindness and hospitality. May the Lord bless you for taking me in and showing kindness to the least of His servants."

He sounded pretentious perhaps, yet looking into his eyes, it was clear Brebeuf meant every word, his words soft like one of their storytellers.

The Iroquois children leaned forward trying to understand his words, the tone of his voice soothing.

Falcon frowned. The white demon was already enchanting the children. He should be left when they moved their camp in the morning. Let him fend for himself. He'd keep Maggie away from this intruder for the remainder of the day, worried an evil spirit would enter their unborn baby as long as Brebeuf remained in their midst.

He glanced up to where his mother was hovering over Maggie, feeding her broth as she lay on their bed. He couldn't question his chief, but he was not going to put his family at risk.

Chapter 11

The further away they moved from the fort, the more Adelaide lost all hope of ever returning home.

"Why won't you let Chief Long Knife love you?"

Maggie raised an eyebrow. Surely she could not be the only one to fall for her captor. She glanced up at Falcon beneath lowered lashes, her cheeks flushing. Oh, he was good to her, his tender loving concealed beneath his iron strength and fierce features.

Adelaide refused to answer the question, looking over at her children shadowing Chief Long Knife. Something stirred in her heart watching her son strut beside the chief, his shoulders straight with an air of confidence in the firm set of his youthful jaw.

Dressed in fringed buckskin, Isabella played with the other children, having picked up the Iroquois tongue quickly. After all these years, Adelaide had no idea her children had an ear for languages.

Sarah sat beside Small Bird, twisting her hands in opposite directions until the kernels of corn released their hold on the cob before falling into the dish. Sarah's soft laughter caused Small Bird to beam in delight.

The Wyandotte Nation highly valued children, physical discipline unheard of. Instead, the children learned by playing and imitating their elders. In this environment, the children thrived and yet, Adelaide worried. After all, their captors were heathens. What influence were they having on her children? What were they telling the kids in a language Adelaide struggled to grasp?

Maggie had clearly already succumbed to Falcon's whiles regardless of the fact he was an unbeliever. No, Adelaide must act quickly resolving to confide in the kindly Jesuit. At the moment, he was the lesser of the two evils.

BREBEUF GLANCED UP in surprise as Adelaide approached. He'd been welcomed into the wigwam after running the gauntlet and given a meal, yet no one had made him leave, prolonging their hospitality to him as they moved camp the day after his arrival.

He was a patient man, repeating their words slowly as he put his mind to learn their language, joining the women out in the fields.

The men laughed behind his back as the demon did women's work, finally realizing Brebeuf was not nearly as evil as they had initially assumed.

The stout man seemed to take great satisfaction in learning their language and, within the month had begun to gain their trust.

Adelaide hunkered down beside the Jesuit as her fingers nimbly harvested roots.

"I am worried..."

Adelaide began looking furtively over her shoulder although she needn't have concerned herself. Maggie was the only one who understood her and she was working at her mother-in-law's side.

Adelaide had Brebeuf's full attention.

"I am worried about my soul and the souls of my children."

The ageing priest nodded, pulling weeds at her side.

"These people are heathens and I fear what they are teaching my children. I am slow to grasp the language..."

"They must be taught the Scriptures. Each is a precious soul facing a Christless eternity..."

"Yes, yes, I know!"

Adelaide was impatient with his slow enunciation. She only had a few minutes before they'd grow suspicious. Adelaide wouldn't put it past thc other young women to report back to her husband. No one could be trusted, except for Maggie and she was so in love with Falcon that Adelaide had begun to second guess her friend as well.

Husband.

The word left a bitter taste in her mouth even as her heart skipped a beat. Ashamed of her heart's reaction at the thought of Chief Long Knife, she pressed forward.

"I cannot be intimate with him. I am married! My husband was left behind..."

Adelaide didn't have to explain. For nearly a month she'd lain in Chief Long Knife's arms, held against his side. The same thing every night - the chief pulling the furs over her shoulders then held her incredibly close until he fell asleep.

Things were changing between them, his eyes on her during the day causing her heart to hammer and his hands on her at night, a silent promise that his waiting had come to an end. She was his wife - completely, and he wouldn't wait much longer.

"If he...it is a sin! I cannot!" Adelaide stammered, glancing up at Small Bird unaware of the scope of her mother-in-law's influence.

"I will speak with your husband tonight. Let us pray the Lord will help me make him understand. You are doing what is right in the sight of the Lord..."

"Thank you," Adelaide smiled at his reassurance.

A year ago she never would have assumed she'd find comfort in the Jesuit's words.

BREBEUF HAD AVOIDED the chief as much as possible, keeping mostly to the women and children. He now mustered courage as he approached the tribe's leader. He wasn't fluent in their language by any means, yet he was certain he knew enough to be able to plead his case.

"I'm Brother Brebeuf," he began, pointing to his sunken chest.

Chief Long Knife glanced at him quizzically. The pale white man in a black woman's dress had made a point to avoid him these many moons. What had changed?

"Chief Long Knife," the towering warrior answered without looking up from the flames.

"Chief Long Knife?" Brebeuf repeated with a shudder, images of how he'd earned the name flitting through his mind.

He was certain to have nightmares now.

"No, I shall call you..." He paused, deep in thought, "Peter. Yes, Peter, it is. It is the perfect name for you. You are a leader and Jesus Christ said to Peter in the Bible, 'Upon this Rock I will build My Church.' Yes, Yes, I claim it in faith - you will be a leader for Christ, souls added to the Kingdom because of you."

Chief Long Knife looked away from the flames, studying the diminutive man before him. He was ranting like a madman.

"Peter...you'll need a last name of course..." *Hendricks.* Brebeuf pulled the first that came to his mind. "Peter Hendricks has a nice ring to it..."

"Is there something you needed?"

Chief Long Knife was finally running out of patience. He had yet to decide on the man they'd rescued from the water.

"Adelaide has been chosen by God for Holy work. You cannot lay with her without incurring the wrath of God. She is married to another."

Brebeuf let his words sink in.

Chief Long Knife raised an eyebrow. Guillaume had been the only man when they'd raided the small village. He'd know. What husband was this weasel of a man referring to?

"There is no husband," Chief Long Knife declared, wanting this conversation to change direction.

"If you are intimate with her, a plague will come and it will be by the hand of God."

Was Brebeuf challenging him?

There was no humour in Brebeuf's eyes as he played on the tribe's natural superstition.

Chief Long Knife lowered his head, not speaking another word. Brebeuf took the hint and shuffled off into the shadows.

Chapter 12

Small Bird could see her son's troubled features from across the lodge. Rising from the farthest side of the room, she joined her son, encouraging him to confide in her what was just said.

"The pale one only wishes to sow discord. Why else does he stay behind with us women instead of being a man and joining your hunts? You were right, my son, he is a demon!"

Small Bird looked over her shoulder at Adelaide, "You've waited too long to fulfill your husbandly duties. Act now before the little man sows further discord among us. Falcon's bride is happy. Dark Star will be happy as well."

"And the curse?"

"There will be no curse, and if the demon has spoken one against you, we will call our shaman and it will be well."

Chief Long Knife nodded, waiting for his mother to retreat before standing. He walked to the door of the wigwam breathing in the cool night air.

Fireflies danced, their lights flickering in the darkness like hundreds of little fairies.

Tonight he would forget Gentle Doe and his child who would have been born by now. His wife likely belonged to another man now and had learned to accept her fate. It was simply the way things were. Chief Long Knife could only hope her new husband was good to her and would raise their son well although only Gentle Doe would ever know the child was meant to become a chief.

Chief Long Knife had only wanted to be considerate of Adelaide and allow himself to grieve over his own loss, but clearly, that had been a mistake. By now she would have been like Maggie, love shining in her eyes instead of fearful resentment. Adelaide may be physically present, but it was clear her heart was far away.

ADELAIDE PUT THE CHILDREN to bed, kissing their foreheads. Without a Bible, she was thankful for the Word of God she had hidden in her heart over the years. Now, it alone sustained her.

"Which memory verse can you remember?" Adelaide whispered in the dark.

"Thou wilt keep him in perfect peace, whose mind is stayed on thee: because he trusteth in thee. Isaiah twenty-six verse three," Joshua whispered in the darkness.

"For God so loved the world that he gave his only begotten Son, that whosoever believeth in him should not perish, but have everlasting life. John chapter three and verse sixteen," Sarah was next.

"Very good. I'm so proud of you!"

"I can't remember Mamma," Isabella admitted, "Can I tell you one in the morning?"

"Sure Honey," Adelaide smiled in the darkness.

"Good night," Chief Long Knife spoke from behind her, startling Adelaide.

How long had he been listening? It was a shame they'd been quoting Scripture in a language he didn't understand. An opportunity lost!

Rising, Adelaide was even more determined to learn the language. If Brebeuf and her son could, there really was no excuse.

Adelaide's thoughts were cut short as Chief Long Knife swept her off her feet, striding towards their bed, a determination in his fathomless black eyes.

ADELAIDE COULDN"T HAVE known Chief Long Knife was such a passionate man. He'd been wild and fierce then so slow and tender until she had done all she could not beg him never to stop when at last he rolled back onto the furs, sweat glistening in the moonlight.

Unable to communicate, he seemed to read her mind, entwining his fingers in her hair before drawing her face down until their mouths merged in a waltz that caused the past to be forgotten - at least for tonight.

Euphoria.

Adelaide's hazy thoughts tried to remember why she'd resisted him for so long. Exhausted, she collapsed in his arms as a soft rumble of laughter interrupted the silence before Chief Long Knife kissed her yet again.

Never had she experienced anything remotely like it, feeling at once the most desired and precious woman in the world, a sensation she most definitely could get used to.

THE NEXT MORNING, ADELAIDE was still laying in her husband's arms when a loud, rhythmic clacking awakened her. Chief Long Knife was always the first to arise, yet this morning, when she opened her eyes, she was still pressed against his heart.

Chief Long Knife awoke with a start, throwing off the furs as he and the other warriors pulled on their loincloths, leaving their wives behind as they ran out the door into the clearing, arrows and war clubs were drawn.

Iroquois raids were much too prevalent, yet instead of the dread enemy, Brebeuf stood in the clearing beside an enormous wooden cross he'd erected just minutes before.

The fool had erected a monstrosity, calling attention to their camp from miles around. The little weasel would be the death of them all!

"Take it down," Chief Long Knife commanded.

"I will not, Peter," Brebeuf stood his ground even as Adelaide stepped outside, enveloped in a long fur blanket, standing at her husband's side.

A shadow passed over Brebeuf's eyes as he realized what had taken place.

"Great destruction will come," he prophesied.

Adelaide shuddered a moment before Chief Long Knife drew her trembling form against his side, offering her his strength.

Chief Long Knife's eyes narrowed, "We are married before the Great Spirit. Take it down."

Brebeuf crossed his arms, "It stays. Come, I want to show you something."

Adelaide pivoted, nearly bumping into Maggie who stood at Falcon's side. An expression passed between the women. Maggie grinned, placing her hand on her round womb.

Brebeuf played his next card, pulling out a worn, dog-eared book from beneath the furs of his pallet. Gently turning the pages, he showed the adults and children horrific pictures of Hell and the nightmarish drawings of the demons who tormented souls for eternity.

Maggie blanched, her legs buckling, yet she flinched at Falcon's touch as he reached out to support her.

Adelaide swallowed hard but didn't move away from her husband. She looked up into his eyes, more determined than ever to see him saved.

"The cross stays," Brebeuf spoke again.

Chief Long Knife nodded. If there was even a hint of truth in those pictures, he wasn't ready to take the risk. This, they must discuss further.

THE VILLAGE SHAMAN eyed Brebeuf with suspicion. He'd received a vision that Brebeuf would destroy them, and since then he watched

Brebeuf's every move. The erecting of the cross was unacceptable, but he was wise enough to know he needed to bide his time.

It came sooner than anyone had thought and in a most unexpected form: There was no rain.

The Huron, as Brebeuf referred to them simply because they resembled wild boar with their unusual headdress, relied on corn as their main food staple. Without corn, they would starve and there could be no corn without rain.

This was the shaman's time to shine, as he rattled turtle shells, calling for the Great Spirit's help. Weeks went by, turning into months and yet there was still no rain.

Chief Long Knife needed to make a decision.

Brebeuf's knees trembled as he approached the chief.

"

"Peter?"

Chief Long Knife didn't respond, so Brebeuf cleared his throat, trying again.

"Peter!"

Chief Long Knife turned, remembering the ridiculous name.

"Peter," Brebeuf began for the third time, "Let me pray now for the rain to come and if my God is the one true God, He will answer with rain."

Like Elijah of old, Brebeuf believed in God for the impossible.

Chief Long Knife was impressed by the tiny man's bold offer. Besides, he had nothing to lose.

Adelaide touched Maggie's arm, "Let's pray with him. Remember how Elijah called down fire from Heaven? This reminds me of then. God must just show His power!"

"Of course!"

Maggie's eyes lit up at the thought of these people seeing God's wonders and putting their trust in HIm.

Falcon and his people had become very precious to her.

Chapter 13

Chief Long Knife had nothing to lose as the tribe gathered for the spectacle, scarcely believing any god would listen to Brebeuf. At best, he was annoying, constantly trying to push the white man's ways and God upon them, yet the shaman hadn't been answered.

Let's see what the tiny man's God can do.

There was an air of anticipation in the hush that ensued.

Perhaps it was a flair for the dramatic, but Brebeuf insisted the cross be taken down and repainted. The colour? A deep, blood red.

Adelaide raised her eyebrow as she glanced at Maggie.

Did God really care that the cross was painted red?

Hardly.

Yet they kept quiet. Brebeuf had spent months with another tribe. Maybe this dramatic display was what was needed to capture the attention of the Wyandotte. If this is what it took for them to understand the sacrifice Jesus made on the cross, then it was well worth it. Brebeuf was simply meeting them where they were in their understanding.

THE WOMEN HELD HANDS as Brebeuf explained the meaning of the red paint and how Jesus, the perfect sacrifice, had been raised up as well, offering Himself for the whole world.

The men were silent, listening to Brebeuf tell them of a Saviour they had never heard of. If he sent rain, this dead man Brebeuf spoke of, still held power.

One thing at a time.

The warriors helped Brebeuf re-erect the red-stained cross, then bowed their heads as Brebeuf prayed that God would send rain, proving to them once and for all that He alone was the true God.

Adelaide squeezed Maggie's hand tight.

This was it.

Nothing.

The heavens were as silent as when the Shaman had cried out to the Great Spirit.

For a moment.

And then the sky grew dark, great drops of water plummeting the parched ground.

The children laughed, dancing in the downpour as the women hurried into the wigwam seeking cover.

Chief Long Knife looked over at Brebeuf but wasn't ready to turn his back on the Great Spirit yet.

"This God of yours is powerful, but it is not our way," Chief Long Knife turned away from the priest.

"The seed has been sown," Brebeuf grinned, undeterred.

"The cross cannot be red," the shaman complained to their chief. "It is frightening the children and will bring us bad luck." He narrowed his eyes, "It looks like the death that will come to us."

Chief Long Knife frowned. He respected the shaman's wisdom.

"We will paint it white in the morning, but the cross will stay."

It was his way of saying thank you to the God who had sent the rain.

THEY HAD SINCERELY believed the miracle of rain would have softened the natives' hearts, proving once and for all that theirs was the one true God. It was not to be.

Over the next few months, the women learned the language, although not yet fluent. Maggie grew round and was heavy with child. An autumn birth seemed likely.

Although Chief Long Knife respected the God who sent the rain, he and the others were insistent that they would never convert. To do so would be to turn their backs on their customs and people. No, a miracle or not, it was not enough.

As a show of appreciation, Chief Long Knife allowed Brebeuf to invite several more Jesuits to join them. They were harmless, as it turned out, and loved to spend time with the children, telling the kids tales they had never heard.

The children listened wide-eyed to Bible stories, even to the oral telling of the catechism.

"One soul," Brebeuf breathed aloud every night as he prayed by his sleeping quarters, "Just one soul, Lord."

The other Jesuits contributed as well, teaching the warriors that their success would only lie in the trading of furs, particularly beaver. If they could trap these mammals, they could trade their pelts at the fort in Quebec for a hefty price. In doing so, they could provide for their people.

Falcon exchanged a look with Chief Long Knife, "If we trade at the fort, we will need to pass through Iroquois territory. It will be our death sentence. Is it worth it?"

Chief Long Knife had been weighing the pros and cons.

"We don't have much choice. We will not live long if we do nothing. Either way, we are dead. If we are successful, our children will see their children."

"When do we leave?"

Chief Long Knife hadn't decided yet. He wanted to learn more. Other than the occasional retaliation raid he had not had much contact with the pale faces. Now, to do business with them, well, he wanted to be prepared.

"I will join you," Brother Andrews promised. "When you leave for the fort, I will join you and will help you negotiate with the traders."

Falcon frowned, his gut feeling warning him the Jesuit wasn't to be trusted.

"We will leave in the morning. Falcon, you will remain here. Your wife will deliver soon and you must stay and protect our people and your child."

Falcon didn't need to say anything. The fort was far and they wouldn't return for weeks.

Brother Andrew's idea proved to be what they needed, the men bringing back simple tools, beads, cloth and seed in exchange for pelts.

Along with the trinkets, they brought back something invisible and much more sinister: Cholera.

The lethal disease swept through their tribe, killing many. It did not differentiate between men, women or children.

Only the pale faces seemed unaffected.

The shaman worked tirelessly, making poultices that had no effect on the European disease the warriors had inadvertently picked up at the fort.

Brebeuf and Adelaide rolled up their sleeves, bringing as much comfort as they could to the dying.

Maggie was taken to a second longhouse, protecting her and the baby from the ravaging disease. Maggie paced the interior, tears tumbling down her cheeks as she prayed for her people. Yet the number of deaths continued to rise.

"Do something!" Chief Long Knife commanded between clenched teeth.

"I am doing all I know to do. I have never seen anything like it!" The Shaman narrowed his eyes glaring at the Jesuits who had recently joined them, "It is a Pale Face disease."

Chief Long Knife looked over at Adelaide. She had been with them for months along with Maggie and they had not grown sick. What if Brebeuf's prophecy was right? Was this the plague he promised would come?

There was no time to dwell on it now, Brebeuf interrupting his thoughts.

"Let me pray and serve these dear souls."

Chief Long Knife nodded. He was better equipped to help the ill, knowledgeable of this disease.

"Trust in Jesus," Brebeuf urged as he bathed their foreheads with fresh river water. "He is your healer. If you do not trust Him and be baptized, you will spend eternity in fire."

The natives did not fully understand the man who showed them compassion, the blazing fever drowning any thoughts they might have.

Those that were able dug the graves, bodies carried out almost hourly.

"Trust Jesus!" Brebeuf's voice was hoarse, tears blinding his eyes. "Don't let it be too late."

"I trust your Jesus," came a feeble whisper.

Brebeuf blinked back tears, smiling down at Thunder Cloud.

"Praise you, Lord! Adelaide, bring me my holy water!"

Adelaide frowned but obeyed Brebeuf's instruction. Using a small dish, he baptized the dying warrior.

They rejoiced over his salvation even as more died that hour.

Miraculously, Thunder Cloud recovered and began urging his brethren to follow his lead and trust Jesus for their salvation.

Brebeuf stood back as others asked to be baptized as well. The seed had borne fruit even in the midst of tragedy.

Chief Long Knife stepped forward, Falcon at his side.

"We trust your God."

Adelaide held a hand up to her mouth, tears dampening her hand as her husband and Maggie's turned their backs on their old ways, accepting the God of Abraham, Isaac and Jacob as theirs.

The shaman's inability to help his people, while Brebeuf's prayers had brought Thunder Cloud back from the brink of death - that had been the turning point they needed. However, not everyone was happy about the change.

Hostility brewed, as of yet, undetected by Chief Long Knife.

Chapter 14

Within weeks, over half the tribe lay buried in shallow graves. Cholera had decimated the Wyandotte Nation and there was absolutely nothing they could do to reverse the events.

To say a heavy cloud of anguish had descended upon the tribe was a great understatement. The piercing cries of the mourners reached the heavens yet there was no comfort to be had.

Chief Long Knife was withdrawn, gazing into the flames for hours at a time, Adelaide observing from a distance. What words could she possibly say to comfort him?

A great, all-encompassing affection filled her heart for these people and the great loss they had suffered, now realizing the ghastly price they paid for the white men, her people, to have come to a land that had never been theirs. An, "I'm so sorry," was not nearly adequate, and she knew it. Small Bird no longer laughed at Isabella's antics, even the children were grave.

"I want to truly be Wyandotte," Maggie murmured as she reached Adelaide's side. "I mean it! I wish I could scrub away my skin!" She glared down at herself with disdain.

"I understand...I feel the same. If only there was something we could do to comfort them," Adelaide whispered.

The men were just babes in Christ - new believers and they were facing a test of faith that would have derailed most modern-day Christians. Adelaide frowned in concern, her unfocused eyes resting on her husband's back. If they became bitter...

"We must go on another raid to replace those we lost," Chief Long Knife did not look up at the rows of empty beds, the silence in the longhouse, deafening.

Adelaide gasped, covering her mouth. She remembered all too well their last raid, she and Maggie being their victims.

Those men that remained nodded. There was no time to lose.

"We will not attack the French," Chief Long Knife directed, "They have shown us mercy during this sickness and we owe much to the little man."

"Then where?" they leaned forward, hanging on their chief's words.

"To the south."

It was all they needed to know. The Jesuits and women had learned their language. Chief Long Knife wouldn't say more in front of them.

"We leave at dawn."

The few surviving warriors agreed. Brother Andrew stepped forward, no longer frightened of the natives. They were no longer savages in their eyes.

"If you will receive Christ as your Saviour, we will make sure our people supply you with guns...rifles."

Chief Long Knife leaned forward. His people only used war clubs, bows and arrows or tomahawks. The Iroquois used rifles when they raided their villages, easily killing his people who didn't stand a chance when faced with their deadly aim, fleeing at the sound of gunpowder. This would be a game-changer.

AS THE CHIEF'S WIFE, Adelaide calmly approached her husband, placing a gentle hand on his sinewy forearm. She'd read of this when teaching her children their history lessons. The Dutch settlers had given the Iroquois the first guns, pitting them against the French and then the English. It would not end well if they obtained guns too. She must protect her people.

Chief Long Knife concealed his surprise instantly, turning his attention to his wife. The women were the leaders of the tribe, guiding with their wisdom. Adelaide clearly loved his people, having proven it as she attended the dying.

"Salvation cannot be bribed," she murmured, her voice low as she gazed up into his eyes, "It is by faith we are saved. To say you are a Christian merely to be able to have a rifle...it will not count in the hour of death."

Maggie nodded, reaching for Falcon's hand.

Chief Long Knife was aware he did not know much about this new God, but what he did know was his people were on the verge of being wiped out. Yet, if his wife disagreed with Brother Andrew, he would have no part in it.

"We will trust this God to protect us. No, we will not accept your offer."

Brother Andrew frowned but held his tongue. Chief Long Knife didn't speak for everyone. Rifles, they would have.

Brebeuf was on the fence, finally speaking, "Our people, the French will be your allies. You have my word. In exchange for your conversions, as Brother Andrew has said, you will receive rifles to better defend yourselves. It will be our gift."

He knew they realized it would be inappropriate to refuse. He had written back to Quebec, and in turn to France, that of all the tribes they encountered, the Wyandotte were by far the most civilized and therefore, tranquil. Now that they were open to the Gospel... Yes, they must work together.

The French were great in number, yet most were fur traders. They did not make homesteads, stealing land that was not their own. Rather many chose to live like the natives and adopt their ways, even marrying women from the tribes they befriended. The French were not a threat.

In contrast, the English were arriving in droves, clearing land, cutting down trees and building homes on stolen land. Little by little, the Native

Tribes were being pushed back by the encroaching white men who had no intention of living harmoniously with natives. It was obvious who their only ally could be.

More than a handful of warriors stood, lining up to be baptized in the name of a God they did not know. They only wanted to be left in peace, yet, if this is what it took to save the lives of their families, yes, they would convert. It was a small price to pay.

"I don't like this one bit!" Adelaide muttered beneath her breath catching Maggie's eye.

It would be so much harder to share the truth with these precious souls now.

Chief Long Knife lowered his voice so only Adelaide could hear.

"We are weakened and have no choice."

Adelaide sighed. Were they really selling their souls?

"Postpone the raid," Brother Andrew smiled as he baptized the last warrior who had stood in line, waiting to be initiated into the new faith. "We will bring you the rifles as we promised. It will take a few weeks..."

"We don't have that time," Chief Long Knife cut him short. "If the Iroquois attack us now, we will not survive. We must grow our numbers before they discover our weakened condition. When we return, have the guns here."

JAIRA PLUNGED HER HANDS into the dirty, tepid water before rubbing homemade lye soap over the white shirt she held in her hand. At least it had been white long ago, a brown stain on the collar and patches betraying its age. Jaira prided herself in her hard work and thriftiness.

"Do you think our husbands will return today? It's been mighty long since they left to squash that uprising..." Elizabeth didn't need to finish her sentence.

"I don't know, but I swore I heard a warcry last night on the other side of the wall. They're waiting for us, I just know it!" Jaira's anxiety rose as she described an almost certain attack.

"No, I don't think anyone would be foolish enough to try to make it past the Iroquois. It is a good thing we made an alliance with them, that's what! But you're right, I'll feel safer when John returns."

Jaira wasn't in a rush for William to return. He was an insolent, withdrawn man. At least, that is how he behaved when they were alone. In front of others, he was as charming as could be, never revealing his true colours. Jaira's thoughts were a tangled mess. If he never returned, she would finally be free.

"Have mercy," she quickly repented, hoping God would overlook that small slip up.

She tried to push the thought from her mind. If William never returned, she would be finally free to marry one of the soldiers who guarded the fort. A blonde, a red-head, it really wouldn't matter. Just maybe, for the first time in forever, she would be reminded what love was.

Smoke seeped beneath the walls of the fort, a distraction. Attention on the fire igniting the hewn logs, they did not notice the warriors climbing the barrier until it was too late. Shrill war cries filled the air a moment before those that had remained behind at the fort were taken captive, the wooden defence burned to the ground.

Muffling the screams of the captive women with muscled hands, they dragged their plunder to the river where the canoes bobbed gently on the water.

Chief Long Knife stood at the front of his canoe. He had not taken any captives, watching as his men claimed pale faces and a few Iroquois to replace those that cholera had taken from them. Appeased, they headed home, turning south to avoid any Iroquois on their way. Once these captives had been adopted into the tribe, they would be ready to defend themselves. Until then... silence.

Strong Oak removed his hand from Jaira's mouth. His wife had died just two weeks earlier. His chief and Falcon were happy with their pale women. He avoided the fierce stare of the Iroquois woman his brother had caught. No, he'd settle with the green-eyed woman. He was in no frame of mind to endure a fight. There was something in Jaira's eyes that he understood. She wouldn't fight her fate, he could bet on it.

Chapter 15

Returning home, the Wyandotte gathered relieved to see their men return safely. Clearly, the raid had been successful.

Small Bird smiled, nudging the women forward, "You will have sisters now. It is our way, bringing into our tribe those who will take the place of the ones we lost. That is why you are here..."

Adelaide had never thought to ask that question...

"The Iroquois attacked us, taking all the young women and children. Our men raided your town to replace those they had lost..."

Adelaide's eyes narrowed. Had Chief Long Knife been married? She was his replacement wife? A pang of hurt whispered at her heart, not for his loss, but that he had once loved another.

"Will you join us?" Maggie's mother-in-law passed out sharp sticks, forgetting at that moment Maggie still had not forgotten what her first husband had endured. It was bad timing.

"Of course not! Why would you want to hurt these men?" Maggie's cheeks flushed as her temper rose.

"Their spirits must be broken if they are to be part of our tribe. We cannot risk them rising against us," Small Bird shrugged, but seeing the pain in her daughter-in-law's eyes, she held back, not joining with those who were forming a gauntlet.

Chief Long Knife did not notice, striding to the end of the line. He didn't raise a war club or a stick, his eyes narrowing as he fingered his knife. He knew what was necessary. None of these men must ever attack them. They couldn't risk having an enemy in their midst.

Jaira closed her eyes in horror as one after another, the men she knew who had been left behind to man the fort were forced to run the gauntlet, beaten until they were bloodied and broken. Then, one by one, the chief sliced their fingers. Those that howled in pain were scalped, their carcasses cast to the side for now.

Maggie bit back tears as the stack of bodies piled up.

"Only the brave may become Wyandotte," Small Bird explained.

Cowardice would get them killed.

Adelaide turned her head, vomiting at the sight. Small Bird clucked her tongue. They may speak the language, but their fortitude was weak. Leading Adelaide and her friend away from the sight, the women returned to their children within the longhouse. Chief Long Knife would regret his actions tonight, Adelaide promised.

BREBEUF GRIMACED BUT said nothing as the captive men were separated. Those who hadn't flinched to the right and those that had screamed in pain, well, they were added to the pile to be buried later. He had done his research and knew what was coming next. Straightening his shoulders he swallowed hard, asking God for boldness he simply did not have.

"Peter," he interrupted the chief, "You cannot eat these men." Gesturing to the ones who had endured the first round of torture. "You are a Christian now - a child of God. We do not eat each other."

Chief Long Knife raised an eyebrow then nodded, acknowledging he had heard Brebeuf's instruction. He hadn't intended to feast on flesh - not today. These men were to be adopted into the tribe, yet he held up his hand, repeating what Brebeuf had told him.

"We no longer eat our captives. It is against our new God's ways. From this day forward, it will not be done in my tribe."

Black Bear scowled. Chief Long Knife was letting a little Frenchman lead him around by the nose. This was just one step in Chief Long

Knife leading the tribe away from their traditions. He was treading on dangerous ground.

Adelaide watched with narrowed eyes as the women were escorted into the longhouse, an unnerving twisting in her stomach as she witnessed the same expression of hopelessness in their eyes that had been reflected in her face only a few months before.

SHE KNEW SHE SHOULD show more empathy, perhaps a sprinkle of Christian charity would help. After all, she and Maggie were the only ones who spoke their language: English. Maggie's was broken but Adelaide, well, it was her native tongue.

Her youngest pranced around Chief Long Knife's legs, blissfully oblivious of how barbaric her stepfather had been not yet an hour ago. She couldn't endure the thought of him touching Isabella's head, frigid tingles exploding up her spine.

Maggie grinned, waddling over to where the women sat huddled together, fear in their eyes.

"I'm Maggie," she smiled warmly, pointing to herself.

Jaira knew just enough French to get by, recognizing instantly Maggie's thick accent. She thought she had seen the last of those French frogs when she accompanied her husband farther south...apparently not. Were they back in Canada? She'd lost all sense of direction as they were carted off like sacks of potatoes to this godforsaken village.

Maggie was persistent or annoying - whichever word you chose to describe her would fit perfectly.

"Come, I know it isn't much but you must be starving. There is fresh corn mash in the pot. If you don't eat, you'll waste away and that won't do at all. You are valuable, you know. If you prove your worth, you will make it..." she glanced over at Falcon, "You might even begin to be happy here."

Jaira rolled her eyes as she grimaced, trying her best to hide her chagrin.

Really? How could this woman even think they could hold food down after watching too many of their male friends murdered before their eyes?

"No thanks," Jaira answered for the others.

We'll just wait. Our husbands will come looking for us and when they do, you'll all regret what happened here today.

Maggie glanced over at Adelaide, wordlessly imploring her friend to do something - comfort these women and help them adjust - it was the right thing to do.

Adelaide didn't move a muscle. She was painfully shy, to begin with, but that wasn't the reason. Well, not exactly. She sat beside Small Bird, joining the Native women as they observed the huddling white women from a distance.

Maggie frowned, then continued.

"It really isn't so bad. It took Adelaide and I a little while to adjust and even longer to learn the language. I accepted my fate sooner so it was much easier on me, but Adelaide was far more stubborn. I'd recommend you accept the inevitable. There is no point in fighting it. I am assuming you are Christian as well? Our chief Chief Long Knife," she indicated to the man who stood leaning against one of the main poles, "He is a believer and so is my husband. See? I told you it isn't so bad here. Then there is Brebeuf - he is the bald Jesuit. The others, well, they come and go so it doesn't matter if you don't learn their names right away...."

Was she talking too much? It had to be her nerves.

Jaira scowled, translating. The man who had sliced all the males' fingers was a Christian? Hardly! And as for the bald Jesuit - he could stay exactly where he was. Jaira would never be a Catholic and she didn't feel much like him harassing her to convert. She had never wanted to see William so badly in her life.

"Thank you for caring," Jaira turned her attention back to Maggie wishing the other woman would stop crouching near them. Maybe she couldn't stand? She looked like she was ready to pop.

Adelaide knew she was being rude. She had to do something, at least say something. Without looking at Chief Long Knife, she stood, crossing the room until she reached Maggie's side.

"I'm Adelaide, and those are my children," she pointed to the three children who had varied shades of blonde hair. They stood out among the Native children, impossible not to see that they had been taken as captives as well.

Jaira's jaw dropped.

"Adelaide? My Adelaide?"

Adelaide frowned, peering closer into the shadows. Her face instantly blanched as she gazed into her younger sister's green eyes.

"What are you doing here? I mean, how did you get here?" Adelaide leaned forward, squatting as well.

"It's a long story..." Jaira hesitated, not sure how much she should say, "but the problem is, we don't know how to get back. After we...um...disappeared, we found ourselves at a fort where we have been for the past few months. What about you? How long have you been in this place?"

"I'm not sure. I'm guessing at least a few months," Adelaide glanced down at Meg's extended stomach, "More than a few months..."

"How?"

"Arlana sent me this odd-looking Mohawk necklace. I put it on my desk and started the children's next lesson when the fan started blowing harder and the next thing I knew, I was in a church service in this...century? Brother Brebeuf was preaching. Maggie and...."

Adelaide stopped herself short, "Anyway, they invited us to have dinner with them when we were attacked."

She didn't have to explain further.

Jaira looked at Maggie differently. She knew her sister well enough to know which parts she had purposely left out.

"Oh, I'm so sorry!" Jaira murmured, smiling sadly at Maggie.

The poor woman wasn't intending to be bothersome, she was apparently just very lonely.

"William is a soldier now. He left a few weeks ago to help the English deal with some squirmish. I was hoping he was going to return today..." Jaira didn't complete her sentence.

Adelaide shook her head, empathizing with her sister.

"You won't see him again most likely. They are going to marry you off to one of the men. Apparently, we are replacements for their dead wives. We had cholera hit us this month and..." She glanced over at Chief Long Knife.

Would he be upset she was confiding all their secrets in her sister? She had better be more cautious.

"Anway, the man they will give you to has lost his wife. I know we are still married, but there is no one who is going to rescue us. I fought it for as long as I could, but Chief Long Knife is good to me and the kids."

"Chief Long Knife? That savage brute?"

Adelaide frowned, surprising herself as she grew defensive. Had she grown to love him?

"He is neither of those things! He has loved me more than... No, he just needs to be taught to do better."

"No thanks. You can have him!" Jaira lowered her voice but her features were twisted in a scowl. "I will never give in. It's a sin Adelaide and now I'm seriously worried about you. What are you going to do when you go back to our time? How will you tell Gavin about your unfaithfulness? Have you thought of that?"

Maggie's mother-in-law walked over, assisting Maggie to rise from the floor. She motioned with her hand, trying one of the words she had learned.

"Come."

Reluctantly the woman followed her to the beds she indicated.

"I'll see you in the morning, Jaira," Adelaide lowered her voice, "Don't fight it...."

Then she silently crossed the room, slipping under the furs beside her husband.

Silence.

Dear Reader,

I hope you enjoyed this first book in my series and will leave a review - it would mean so much to me.

Please follow me on Goodreads - I follow back :)

Thank you so much for your support.

Much love,

~ Angeline ~

Don't miss out!

Visit the website below and you can sign up to receive emails whenever Angeline Gallant publishes a new book. There's no charge and no obligation.

https://books2read.com/r/B-A-QGSI-XNRTB

BOOKS2READ

Connecting independent readers to independent writers.

Did you love *Captured Heart*? Then you should read *Fate's Legacy*[1] by Angeline Gallant!

One would give anything to live among the Native Americans while the other wants nothing more than a one-way ticket out of the past.

Unfortunately for Jaira, there is no way out.

Adelaide and George embrace their new lives, but nothing could prepare them for what is coming.

Love, just might not be enough.

Read more at https://www.goodreads.com/author/show/19703964.Angeline_Gallant.

---

1. https://books2read.com/u/m0Eq9J

2. https://books2read.com/u/m0Eq9J

About the Author

Angeline Gallant traces her roots through generations of Old Stock Canadian heritage, her passion for genealogy as deep and enduring as the forests and fields her ancestors once walked. With a reverence for history and an eye for detail, she weaves stories from the fragments of lives left behind in letters, records, and weathered headstones.

An avid reader and devoted writer, Angeline brings the past to life with a curiosity for heraldry and a deep love for the landscapes that shaped her family's story. Each name and date she uncovers feels less like history and more like coming home, a familiar echo in the vast tapestry of time. For her, these stories are not forgotten—they live, breathing in the quiet spaces of memory and tradition, a testament to lives once lived, now eternal in the pages of her books.

Read   more   at   https://www.goodreads.com/author/show/19703964.Angeline_Gallant.

www.ingramcontent.com/pod-product-compliance
Lightning Source LLC
Chambersburg PA
CBHW060442160726
47992CB00003B/1041